PURPOSE IN THE PAIN

ANGELA YARBOROUGH

Love Clones Publishing
www.lcpublishing.net

Printed in the United States of America

First Printing, 2014

ISBN: 978-0692273586

Love Clones Publishing
332 S Michigan Ave – Ste 1032 #N455
Chicago, IL 60604
www.lcpublishing.net

ACKNOWLEDGMENTS

First and foremost I'd like to give honor to God. Lord I thank you for the vision and the gift that you've placed on the inside of me. Without you non of this would be possible. I am ever grateful to you. The more I pour out the more you pour into me. THANK YOU GOD!!! I would also like to thank my many supporters who purchased and read the first book, my very first book. I truly appreciate you all and I love your feedback. So many of you have asked when will the second book be coming out well the wait is over. Here it is and I pray you will like it just as much as the first one. Please continue to support me and keep reading the story gets better and better. And for all you who love the character Curtis he has his own story coming so PLEASE stay tuned. God Bless you all!!!

A New Beginning

Ecclesiastes 7:8 NIV The end of a matter is better than its beginning, and patience is better than pride.

June 5th 2007

Yvette and Tonya and Krystal sat outside on the patio at Tony and Yvette's house, actually it was Tony's house he had moved Yvette in just nine months ago. Tony was now taking care of Yvette. All that talk about him buying her a house she never heard again after they got back to Atlanta. After he won his case against Leonard, he and Yvette became serious and were dating for over a year before he asked Yvette to move in with him. Tony took care of Yvette's every need so she saw no reason to remind him that he said he would buy her a house. So she agreed to move in with him and they began playing house.

Things were going good. As far as Yvette's career was concerned she and Tonya were very popular and their radio station was now #1 in Atlanta. Krystal was still in charge and running things. But this year Yvette, Krystal and Tonya decided they wanted to do more in the promotions business. They sat around the patio table discussing their new venture. They had already chosen a name for their business, Diva Promotions. The ladies were working on a business plan so they could get a business loan to finance the new business. They already had the clientele and were getting new ones every day. The word had spread throughout town about Yvette, Tonya and Krystal. Anyone who was anyone wanted Diva Promotions to host their parties and promote their concerts. They were the first to be called when a new rap artist was coming to town to do a show or concert. And Tony being attached to Yvette helped them out as well. They almost had all of the bugs worked out of their business plan. They were presenting their business plan to the bank for a loan approval the following day. Yvette stretched her arms above her head. "Whew y'all ready to take a break?" Krystal and Tonya had already set back in their chairs. "Yes girl. I think we're just about ready though," Krystal said. Tonya shook her head in agreement. "All that's next is for us to meet with the loan officer tomorrow and present our business plan to him."

"Y'all hungry?" Yvette asked. It was going on 1 p.m. and they had been working since 10 a.m. "Hell yes honey" Tonya said. "Y'all wanna go out and get a bite to eat or do you want me have Rosie to cook up something? "Let's go out" Krystal said. They all agreed. "Let me run upstairs and get my purse and I'll be right back. I'll meet y'all in the front." Yvette ran upstairs to get her purse. She entered their bedroom and looked at herself in the mirror. She was wearing a beautiful strapless sundress; white with hot pink flowers on it and beautiful white sandals to match it. She grabbed her purse and her hot pink sweater, sunglasses and headed back downstairs. Since she had been with Tony she had grown accustomed to the good life. She had nothing but the best. The best clothes and perfume, she drove the best cars and traveled only first class. But Yvette was still the humble good-hearted woman she had always been. She insisted on keeping her independence.

Tony told her she didn't have to work but Yvette insisted on working and making her own money. She tried to contribute to the bills but Tony wouldn't hear of it. Yvette had no need to spend her money. All she had to do was save it in the bank because Tony still put stacks of cash in her hands even though she had her own money. It was almost like he wanted her solely and completely dependent on him. That thought kept coming to Yvette since she moved in with him but she kept pushing it out of her mind. Tony loved her and he wanted to take care of her. He had plenty of money and wanted to share it with her. That's what Yvette told herself every time the thought would creep in her mind. "Ok ladies, let's roll." "Are you driving Yvette? Tonya asked. "Yes I can drive." They all got in Yvette's 2007 pearl white BMW SUV.

They decided to go and have lunch at the Hilton Hotel and spa. Yvette offered to treat the girls to a spa day at the hotel then they would have lunch. Yvette didn't usually go to the hotel for lunch but she frequented it quite often for her spa treatments. So the spa staff knew Yvette very well and she was always welcome as a walk in because she was a big tipper and Tony Riche's girlfriend. The girls were lying on the massage tables in big white plush robes and slippers with towels on their heads. They were getting the works from facials, hair and nails and a massage. They had already gotten their hair washed and had their facials. Now they were waiting for their massages. As soon as the massage therapists entered they went right to work on the ladies. An hour later they were in the salon chairs getting their hair blow dried and styled. The last thing they had done was their pedicures and nails. An hour and a half later they emerged from the spa refreshed and renewed and looking gorgeous. They entered the restaurant and were seated immediately. "Girl I feel so good" Krystal said. "Me too" Tonya agreed. "Thank you for treating us this afternoon" Krystal said. "You're welcome, anytime. It's not like I have anything else to do with my money." Yvette said. "You sound like you regret that" Tonya stated. "Well sometimes I do. When I was married I use to contribute to our household. But Tony has so much money he doesn't need my help. I guess sometimes I feel useless in his life." Yvette said. "Why because he doesn't allow you to pay bills and he takes care of you? Krystal asked. "Yes" Yvette responded. Krystal didn't say anything she wanted Yvette to get the picture and she did. Yvette was her best friend and she just wanted her to be happy. Even though Tony treated her well, she still was not happy. He wasn't spending that much time with her anymore. He was hardly ever home and always on the road. Krystal suspected he was cheating on Yvette but she didn't want to say anything.

After lunch they stopped in the boutique in the hotel and was looking around. "Let's do something tonight" Yvette said to Krystal and Tonya "its Saturday let's go out" Tonya looked at Yvette and said "I'm sorry sweetie I have plans tonight with Steve" Steve was Tonya's main squeeze at the moment. Krystal was still unattached but she was dating. "I don't have anything planned" Krystal said. "You wanna do something? "Sure I'm down with whatever." Tonya was about to speak but she froze in mid-sentence. "Oh hell Naw" Yvette and Krystal stopped talking and looked at Tonya. She was looking out the boutique window at something or somebody. They followed her gaze and immediately saw what she saw. Yvette's mouth fell wide open. She couldn't believe her eyes. This Negro had the nerve to be walking out of the hotel with some floozy on his arms. All three women left the boutique immediately and caught the couple before they got in the car. "Tony!" Yvette yelled. Tony turned around and saw Yvette, Krystal and Tonya and froze. The woman with him stood by his side like she belonged to him. "Baby," He said. "Tony what are you doing? I thought you were out of town? Yvette yelled. "Baby let me talk to you in the car." He said. "No, I'm not getting in no damn car with you. What is this or who is this?" Yvette pointed at the lady. "Baby please just step in the car with me and I can explain." Yvette realized she was making a scene so she agreed to get in the car with him. Krystal and Tonya walked up on ole girl and got in her face looking her up and down. "Um you may as well be gone trick he's with his woman now." Tonya said to the lady "Excuse me? "You heard her" Krystal responded "Be gone, leave, goodbye." She looked at Krystal and Tonya and folded her arms across her chest and rolled her eyes as if to say, "I'm not going anywhere" "Oh you aint gone leave?" Tonya asked. "Ok we'll see about that." Tonya handed her purse to Krystal and took off her shoes and walked towards the woman. She looked at Krystal then at Tonya and took off running down the street. "That's right, be gone heffa." Tonya yelled after her. Krystal was laughing; she and Tonya slapped hands.

Inside the car Yvette was crying and Tony was begging and pleading "Baby don't cry let me explain" He said. "Explain what Tony how you were supposed to be out of town and here I find you walking out of the Hilton with some broad on your arm." "Baby it wasn't like that. We were discussing business." He said. "Well when I asked you who she was why is it she didn't say anything. In fact she stood by your side like she thought she was your woman" Yvette said. "I don't know baby she's the executive type you know that's how they are; too sophisticated to make a scene." Tony said. "Whatever Tony, do you think I'm stupid. I came from a relationship where a man cheated on me regularly so I know the signs." Yvette said. Tony ran his hand through his hair "I'm not cheating on you boo. I love you baby I could never hurt you that way." He said. "Did you go out of town? Yvette asked. "Yeah I just got back earlier than I had planned and I had this meeting to go to this morning so that's why I didn't come straight home. I was gon' call you as soon as I dropped her off." He said. "What is her name? Tony hesitated before he said "Shelly" Yvette rolled her eyes "Just Shelly huh?" Tony sighed and said "Shelly Osborne"

Yvette wiped her eyes and said, "Well can I ask you this? Why is it that you had to drop off Miss Sophisticated Executive? I mean executives usually make enough money to buy their own cars right?

Yvette said. "What company does she work for? "What was your meeting about? Yvette asked. Tony laughed "Baby come on. Why you asking me all these questions? He said. "Because I know you lying to me Tony." Yvette said. Tony scooted close to Yvette and tried to hold her but she pushed him away from her. "Ok let's just go home and finish this conversation alright." He said. "No I drove them here I can't leave them." Yvette said. "Then give Krystal your keys and let her drive your car" Tony said. Yvette handed him her keys. Tony rolled down the limo window and said "Here Krystal can you drive her car home. We'll meet you there." Krystal took the keys from him while giving him the evil eye. She and Tonya both were mean-mugging him. Yvette had told Krystal and Tonya her suspicions of which they didn't doubt because it was obvious since Tony had moved Yvette in; things had died down between them. He was treating her like a wife instead of a girlfriend. Yvette, Krystal and Tonya were inseparable and if you hurt one you hurt them all; that was the pact they made.

Tony had his driver to take them home. Yvette cried all the way there. When they got home he escorted her out of the car and into the house. Yvette snatched away from him once she got in the house. She went right upstairs to their bedroom. Tony followed her. She went directly to their closet but instead of going to her side of the closet she turned the corner that separated the closet and went on his side. She started pulling out his drawers and looking through his jewelry boxes. Tony walked in behind her and asked "What are you doing Yvette? "I'm looking for evidence." Tony laughed he stepped in front of her and his drawer. "What's wrong? You got something to hide? She said. "No but you are acting childish" He said. "Oh I'm acting childish now? Yvette asked. "Yeah you are" Tony said. Yvette walked away from Tony and left him in the closet. He followed her out "Now do you want to talk like an adult or do you want to continue to fight and argue? He asked. "Well I'm listening Tony go ahead and speak? Yvette said. "What I told you is the truth baby. I didn't make that up." He said. Yvette was pacing back and forth. "Look at you looking all beautiful; you too fine to be acting like this baby." Tony said.

"Tony don't even go there with me. I know you lying." Yvette said. Tony walked toward Yvette and grabbed her around the waist and pulled her to him. "Aw baby don't be that way. I love you." He said. Tony tried to kiss her but she moved her head and pushed his face away with her hand. He let her go and she moved away from him and sat on the bed. Tony walked over and sat down beside her. He put his arm around her waist again. "Baby I can understand that you upset but please believe me when I tell you I love you. You are the only woman for me." He said. Yvette looked at Tony and yelled "I know you love me Tony. I'm not disputing that. But I'm disputing the bullshit story you gave me."

She said. Tony held his head down "Look Yvette I promise she is just a friend ok. There is nothing between us. I was at the hotel for a meeting and we saw each other and we were going out to eat that's all." He said. "Oh I thought you said it was a business meeting and if you just saw her at the hotel why did you have to drop her off? I mean how was she gone get home if she hadn't saw you" Yvette yelled. "And why would you be going out to eat when there's a restaurant right there in the hotel?" "I don't know Yvette damn I'm sorry. Please can you forgive me? Tony said. "No Tony I can't! You know I sit around this big ass house bored to death waiting on you to come home. When you do come home you don't even call me and then I find you preparing to spend time with another woman. What am I supposed to do? Yvette said. "I understand you're lonely but I have fights and business that requires me to travel a lot."

He said. "You use to take me with you" Yvette said. "Is that what this is about? You wanna come with me while I'm on the road? What about your job baby? He said. "Tony I know I can't go on the road with you. But I just don't feel like part of your life anymore!" Yvette said. Tony stood up and held his arms out and said, "How don't you feel a part of my life Yvette? I gave you all of this. You the only woman I ever asked to live with me; doesn't that tell you something? I love you and you'll probably be my wife someday." Tony said. Yvette turned and looked at Tony "Probably" She said. "Here we go with this" Tony said. "No it's no problem Tony I'm not asking you to be my husband; I just want a little more intimacy from you. We use to spend a lot of time together." Yvette said. "I don't know what else I can say Yvette" Tony said. "What if when you come home you don't find me here? Yvette said. "What is that supposed to mean you leaving me? Tony said. "I'm just saying what if I get as busy as you are and I'm never here for you? What then, would you understand? Or what if the shoe was on the other foot; what if it was me who you seen getting in the car with another man? Yvette asked. Tony looked Yvette in her eyes "What you saying you cheating on me? He asked. "No Tony I just want to know what your reaction would be." Yvette said. Tony rubbed his head and said, "You know the only time a woman say shit like that is if she's cheating or thinking about it." He said. "Ain't nobody cheating. I guess I'm just curious as to how you would handle the situation." Yvette said. "I would be pissed and ready to kill somebody. You cheating on me? He asked. "I said no" Yvette said. "Don't ever do that!" Tony said. "Do what Tony? Yvette asked. "Cheat on me; don't ever let me catch you with another man Yvette." Tony said. "Tony I would never cheat on you baby I love you." Tony and Yvette embraced each other "Yvette you mean the world to me baby." Tony hugged her tighter "You mean the world to me too" Yvette responded.

They made love and all was right with the world again. Krystal and Tonya had dropped Yvette's car off and left. They knew the routine between the two of them. They didn't even bother to knock on their bedroom door because they knew they were in the bed. It was 7:00 p.m. when Yvette and Tony emerged from their bedroom. They had showered and were lounging in their robes in the kitchen. Rosie their housekeeper and cook fixed them a beautiful supper. They took turns feeding each other and kissing in between bites. After dinner they went back to their bedroom and watched TV cuddled in each other's arms until they fell asleep. The next morning Yvette was up before Tony. She showered and got dress for the meeting they had with the loan officer from the bank. Yvette had to meet Krystal and Tonya at the bank at 9:00 a.m. Yvette kissed Tony on his forehead as he lay asleep in the bed before she left.

She rushed out of the house and got in her truck and took off. Yvette called Krystal on her way to the bank "Hey Kris, where are you? "Hey Yvette, I'm on my way to the bank. Are you there already? Krystal asked. "No I'm just heading out now. What about Tonya?

Yvette asked. "I spoke to her she's on her way as well so we should all be there about the same time. So how did everything go yesterday? Krystal asked. Yvette smiled when she thought of her sweetheart "It went ok" "So what did he have to say for himself? Krystal said. "He said she was an old friend he had run into after his meeting at the hotel and when we saw them they were going to get something to eat and catch up basically." Yvette said. "And you believe him?" Krystal asked. "I didn't at first but I don't know. I still have my guard up." Yvette said. "If she was just a friend then she wouldn't have stood there like she did yesterday. If their relationship was platonic she would have understood and walked away but no she didn't do that. Tonya had to practically run her off with her shoe yesterday." Krystal said. Yvette started laughing, "She did" Yvette said. "Girl yes, that heffa was looking like she was gone wait 'til Tony got out of that car so they could continue whatever it was they were about to do. In other words she was letting you know that she's not going anywhere no matter what he tell you.

If Tonya wouldn't have ran her away she would have stood there until Tony got out of that car. She's more than a friend Yvette don't believe the hype boo." Krystal said. Yvette sighed she figured as much but she wanted to give Tony the benefit of the doubt since she had never before caught him cheating. Her spirits went completely down again. She was happy when she woke up this morning having spent a glorious night in the arms of the man she loved. But she knew she had to face reality her man was cheating on her and he had lied to her about it. "Yvette… you alright? "Yeah I will be." "Well, look Yvette don't think too much on it. Don't let this stress you out. Pray about it and give it to God sweetie. You'll get through this." "Yeah, you're right. I guess I'll see you at the bank then. Bye." Yvette disconnected the call. She was really hurt. She wasn't trying to be rude to Krystal but she didn't feel like talking anymore. "Here I go again." Yvette thought back on what she went through with Leonard. But at least he's not hitting me. I know he loves me. He takes good care of me and let me move in with him. Why should I give him up and let this other woman have him. He has stuck by my side through thick and thin and he said maybe or probably he would marry me some day. Yvette thought to herself. I know what Krystal is saying is true but my situation could be a lot worse.

I'll speak to Tony when I get back or maybe I'll just let it go and see if he slips up again. If I confront him again he'll only lie to me so it's best to let him think I've forgotten about it and that I believe him. Yvette thought back to a year and a half ago to when she first met Tony. She vowed she wouldn't allow a man to take her identity from her ever again. And for the most part he hadn't, except that she allowed him to move her into his home and started taking care of her. She remembered having a problem with the way he just took control over everything; it mirrored her marriage so much aside from the abuse it scared her. How did I get from there to here? Yvette thought to herself. "I allowed myself to fall in love that's how!" she said out loud. But this is not a bad relationship. I have a beautiful place to live and I don't want for nothing except his companionship and intimacy. I have intimacy from him when he's home. Hmm, sex is not intimacy Yvette; it's just sex. A lot of women would kill to have what I have. Tony is a good man. Yvette was thinking to herself. But even as she thought it, she knew it was just a copout rather than face the truth about her situation.

The truth is he didn't appreciate her. Tony had slid Yvette right in the position he had planned for her; house wife without the marriage. While he played the field and had her at home whenever he felt like spending time with her. Sure he treated her good as far as taking care of her and putting money in her pocket but what was the tradeoff? She was left home in a big house with no one to talk to except her friends but they had their own lives and weren't always available and why should they be when she lived with her man. I thought that was the point of him moving me in here so we could be together. She thought to herself.

Yvette pulled up in front of the bank. She got out of the car and walked inside. When she entered the lobby of the bank she saw Tonya sitting in the waiting area. She walked over and sat next to her. "Good Morning sweetie" Yvette sat her purse down and said "Good morning" sounding sad. That made Tonya look at her "What's wrong boo? Tonya asked. "It's not a good morning." Yvette said. "Did you and Tony get everything worked out? Tonya asked. "Yeah we did." She said. Yvette didn't say anything else. Tonya looked at her waiting for a response "Sooo… is everything alright? Tonya asked. Yvette tried to put a smile on her face "Yes its fine." She said. Krystal walked in "Hey ladies" They both spoke at the same time. Krystal hugged Yvette "I know I made you mad girl but I was just keeping it real with you." She said. "I know you were, it's just that I wasn't in the mood to hear it this morning. I'm sorry for being rude and hanging up like that." Yvette said. "Aw girl, you don't have to apologize I understand and I know you didn't mean it. But look it's time to get our game faces on. We're going to walk in there and get this loan because we are dunamis women of power, mind and strength in Jesus Name!" Krystal said. They all agreed and held hands as Krystal said a quick prayer.

Heavenly Father, Lord we thank you right now for allowing us to be here today. We know that it is only you that has brought us this far and we know it's you who is going to see us through this business venture. We thank you for what you have allowed us to go through that has prepared us for this day. We thank you because we know that You are our Sheppard and we shall not want as long as we hold on to your unchanging hands. Lord we ask you to forgive us of our sins this day. Lord we ask you to wash us clean and make us whole this day in Jesus name. Lord we ask for your favor this morning. We ask that your will be done. Lord you know the desires of our heart and you also know what we need better than we do. You know it is our desire that we get this business loan but we ask above all things that your will be done not ours. If for some reason we shall not get the loan Lord we will know it was not in your will and we will accept that. We ask that you continue to provide for us and make a way out of nowhere. In Jesus name Amen.

They all sat down next to each other holding hands. No sooner had they sat down, the loan officer came and introduced himself. The ladies walked confidently behind Mr. Leland into his office. Behind the closed door Mr. Leland began to look over their business plan. The women sat silently as he read over their plan. Finally he looked up and said it looked good. "I'll go ahead and submit your loan for approval. Now I can't guarantee it will be approved of course you know that but I'll recommend you for the loan. I believe this is a good business venture and is likely to be a success; based on the skills you all have and your experience in the industry." The ladies were excited and smiling. They went over a few more mandatory details and paper work for the submission. They also discussed their rate and interest. Within the hour the meeting was over and the Divas were walking out of the bank floating on cloud nine and ready to go and celebrate. They went and had breakfast at their favorite café and discussed their business strategy. "I think it would be a good idea for us to keep it the way it is. Me and Tonya dealing with the celebrities and you Krystal handling the business side of it." Yvette said. "Well I would like to get in on the celebrity side of it to." Krystal said. "Why don't we all just handle everything together? Tonya stated. "Ok let's all handle the celebrities together but we all have our area of expertise.

Like I believe Krystal is good at handling the business because that's what you do and I believe Tonya would be good with handling the celebrities because out of all of us she is the most outgoing. And me well I don't know" Yvette said. Tonya spoke up "You are good with handling the celebrities as well you just have a different approach than I do. And the men seem to flock to you. They're attracted to that innocence you seem to have and that's a good thing." Tonya said. "I agree," said Krystal. "Ok then, it's settled we'll all work the celebrity side together and pretty much work our areas of expertise. I believe that we'll all learn from each other anyway. And I believe it's good for us all to know each side of the business so we can all run it alone if we ever have to." Yvette said. "That's right" Krystal agreed. "That's a good idea." Tonya stated. Yvette held up her glass of orange juice and said, "Let's toast to Diva's Promotions" Krystal and Tonya held up their glasses and they tapped their glasses and drank.

Yvette pulled into the driveway at home. As she walked through the front door she was still thinking of her meeting with her girls. Yvette was still a little upset about what she discussed with Krystal regarding Tony but for the most part she was excited about their business. She ran up the stairs to the bedroom looking for Tony. As she entered the bedroom she saw he wasn't in there. Yvette put her purse down and her keys and went back down stairs to the kitchen. "Hola Rosie, have you seen Tony?" Rosie spoke with a slight Hispanic accent "Yes mam, he is working out in the weight room" Yvette went downstairs to the recreation area where in one room Tony had it laid out like a club with a bar and bar stools. He had round tables set up with little dimmed lit lamps he even had a dance floor and a DJ booth. There were couches and chairs for lounging and a big screen television above the bar and a projector screen built in the ceiling. He also had mirrors surrounding the dance floor. Upon entering this room you were immediately transformed from a house setting to the club scene. In the other room there was a pool table and three video games like the ones you would find in an arcade.

There was of course Pac Man, Mortal Combat and Tetris. There was a big stereo system and a big screen television as well as a smaller television if anyone wanted to play the play station or Xbox he had in the room; there were also two flat screen computers with Internet access. This was clearly a room for children to use to keep them occupied when the adults wanted to party. And finally there was a fully equipped gym room complete with an indoor track. Tony also had an indoor pool and an indoor basketball court on the other side of the house. Yvette opened the door to the gym room. She knew Tony was in there because she could hear his rap music playing. He always worked out to music, mostly rap. Tony didn't hear Yvette open the door and walk in. He was sitting with his back towards her on the weight bench; he was on his cell phone. "Baby I wasn't trying to play you. I didn't know my woman would be there" He said. "I'm not gone tell her about you she wouldn't be down with this" He said. "Look I already told you I'm not about to leave my woman for nobody. I made that perfectly clear to you in the beginning. She's always gone be number one in my life; so stop thinking you gone to take her place" Tony said.

"Hey you number two that's it and that's all. And as you well know the number one always comes first" Tony said. "I can't do nothing about that. That's the risk you take when you mess with somebody else's man. You knew the risk as well as I did" Tony said. "Be happy in the position you in, ok" He said. Yvette stood there listening to his whole conversation. The excitement she felt about her new business venture was gone; replaced with anger and pain. "Look stop giving me all this grief. I don't have to put up with this shit. Like I said many a' times, I have a woman and I can get this bullshit from her I don't need it from you too." Tony said and hung up the phone. He looked up and saw Yvette was standing behind him in the mirror. He looked surprised hoping she hadn't heard any of his conversation. Tony turned around slowly and nervously "Hey baby, how did your meeting go at the bank? He said. Yvette didn't say anything she just stared at him trying hard to fight the tears welling up in her eyes. Tony knew then that she had heard every word. He saw the tears about to fall from her eyes. "Baby don't do that. You know I can't stand to see you cry" Tony said. Yvette swallowed before she spoke hoping her voice wouldn't crack "If you don't like to see me cry then you should stop doing the things that brings tears to my eyes" She said. Yvette turned and walked out of the weight room. She ran up the stairs as fast as she could but Tony was right behind her. He caught up to her and grabbed her around her waist. Yvette was screaming and crying yelling at Tony to let her go.

Tony ran up the stairs with Yvette dangling in his arms. He came out of the basement and walked to the stairs that led to their bedroom. He ran the length of the stairs never faltering with Yvette in his arms. Once inside their bedroom he closed the door behind them and threw Yvette on their bed. Yvette slid a little as she hit the bed. Her heart began to beat fast because she remembered the last time Leonard threw her across a bed it resulted in her hitting the floor and him walking toward her to beat her. Yvette sat up quickly as Tony walked toward her "I don't know how much you heard but you did hear me tell her I had a woman" Tony said. "You lied to me again, Tony." Yvette said. She couldn't hold back the tears any longer. Tony sat down next to Yvette and said "Baby don't cry. I'm sorry. You heard me tell her you're number one in my life and I meant that. I never lied to her or promised her anything. I love you baby." Tony said. "NO YOU DON"T LOVE ME Tony. If you loved me you wouldn't be putting me through this." Yvette said. "Come on baby I made a mistake and I'm sorry. Women throw themselves at me all the time. It's hard when you have that much attention from women Yvette. I think I've been good. Usually I don't even try to be faithful to any woman in my life. I love you girl that's why I haven't had any other woman until now.

I made a mistake Yvette please forgive me baby!! Please!!" Tony was on his knees in front of Yvette begging. She thought about what Tony said and she believed him when he said he had not been with any other woman except Shelly. Leonard cheated on her all the time and treated her much worse than Tony treats her. She decided to give her man another chance. "Tony I left an abusive marriage because I wanted a better life for myself. Now here you are doing some of the things I vowed I would never put up with again. I love you and I'm a good woman and I deserve a good man." Yvette said. "You right baby you do deserve a good man. And I am a good man baby I just made a mistake. Just give me another chance." Tony pleaded. "Tony I'm so tired of being hurt and let down" Yvette said. "I know you are sweetie and if you give me a chance I'll make it up to you. I promise" Tony said. "Tony you get her ass on the phone right now and you tell her it's over between the two of you. DO IT NOW" Yvette said.

Tony didn't hesitate to pick up the phone then he realized he didn't know her number by heart. He said "I'll be right back I have to go and get my cell phone." Tony ran out of the bedroom and down the stairs. Yvette sat on the bed waiting for him to get back. I must be out of my mind to be settling for this. But I love him and he's not really that bad. Plus he deserves a second chance. I gave Leonard a lot of chances why not give this man at least one more. She told herself. Tony came back in the bedroom with his cell phone in his hand. He scrolled down the contact list and called Shelly back. "Hey Shelly, I'm sorry about hanging up on you earlier. I just called to let you know I can't see you anymore; it's over. I told you I had a woman and I'm not gon' continue to hurt my girl over you. I love her and I'm gon' be with her and only her. Please don't call me anymore and I won't call you." Yvette could hear Shelly yelling at Tony through the phone. "I'm sorry Shelly but it is what it is. I love my girl and that's it. I never led you on. Well I have to go. Like I said it's over you don't have to call me anymore. Good bye." Tony closed his phone and threw it on the bed. "See, I promise baby it's only you from now on." He said. Tony got down on his knees and hugged Yvette's waist and laid his head in her lap as she sat on the bed.

Los Angeles - June 15th 2007

Curtis sat anxiously in the bleachers of the high school gymnasium. He watched her march in the gym wearing her cap and gown along with the other hundreds of students on their graduation day. He was so proud of Ashley. He could hardly believe this day had finally come. Although, Ashley was graduating a year early because she was so smart and had earned more than enough credits. It seemed like yesterday that he was changing her diapers and wiping her mouth and cleaning her nose. They grow up so fast. In the fall Ashley would be attending Florida State. She was so excited and of course Curtis had to foot the bill for her tuition but he didn't mind; he would do anything for his baby. Tears welled up in his eyes as he watched her walk across the stage and accept her diploma. Curtis stood up holding the video camera in his hand as she walked. Curtis sat in the middle of his mother and sister. Marissa sat next to his mother and Lil Curtis sat on the side of his aunt Krystal. When the last student walked across the stage and accepted his diploma the principal congratulated all students and announced the class of 2007.

All the graduates stood up and threw their hats in the air. Curtis and the rest of his family made their way to floor to hug Ashley. Curtis reached her first and grabbed her. He hugged her so tight. Ashley hugged her father back but when she tried to let go he held her tighter "Um dad you're hurting me" Ashley said. Curtis kissed her on the cheek and said, "I'm sorry baby. I'm so proud of you" Marissa came forward and hugged her. Curtis watched her she was looking beautiful as usual and damn sexy. Curtis tried not to look too much. He didn't want her to think he was still attracted to her. Marissa stepped away from Ashley to give the others a chance to congratulate her. Curtis had them all to get in a group so he could take pictures. When he was done taking pictures he asked Krystal to take a picture of him and Ashley then of him Ashley and his son. Curtis took them all out to lunch after the graduation to celebrate and later that night he was giving Ashley a big pool party at his house. He couldn't wait to give her the gift he got for her.

He bought her a brand-new 2007 red drop top Mustang. Ashley always wanted her own car but Curtis refused to get her a car of her own while she was in high school. He allowed her to drive his wife old car a 2003 BMW. It wasn't old by any means but it was old to them because they always drove brand new cars. Curtis wanted her to take the car with her to school so she would have a way to get back and forth while living on campus. He was going to give it to her when they got back home before the party started.

Curtis couldn't wait to see the look on her face. He really was proud of her; they'd had a rough time during the divorce but they both handled it well and he wanted to reward her. Curtis was dating a woman named Lisa now and both of his kids seemed to like her. Marissa was always interfering in his relationship. In fact the last woman he dated was Kristine. Marissa ran her off with her nonstop requests and demands on Curtis to do things for her. Of course it was done on purpose because she wanted the woman to think he was still involved with her. So far so good with Lisa, Marissa hadn't sabotaged his relationship with her yet.

Back at Curtis's house Krystal and her mother were busy with the caterer getting everything set up for the party. Curtis was in his office writing out checks for the caterer and DJ. Ashley was in her room on the phone and Lil Curtis was in the family room playing video games. By 5:00 p.m. everything was ready for the big pool party. The caterer was out on the patio barbequing and preparing other dishes for the party. Krystal and Curtis were sitting in his office talking "So how's everything going sis? He asked. "Everything is actually going well. We got the loan and were in the process of lining up gigs." Krystal said. "That's good I'm proud of you sis." Curtis said. "Thank you, it feels good to own my own company. I know it's not big right now but I believe were gonna be very successful." She said. "So when do I get to meet your business partners? Curtis said. "Whenever you get out to Atlanta" Krystal responded. "Which probably won't be soon I have so many dates lined up for my groups. I'll be on the road for a while." Curtis said. "Well that's good you guys are getting booked; getting gigs." Krystal said. "Yeah it is." He said. "How's things on the love front? Krystal asked. "I knew that was coming." Krystal laughed. "It's going good." Curtis said. "And" She asked. "And what?" Curtis responded. "And who is she? Krystal said. "Her name is Lisa" Curtis said. "Ooww Lisa. Is she pretty?

Krystal asked. "You know it. I don't date anybody that's ugly." Curtis said. Krystal laughed again "You a mess" She said. "I need to meet her to see if I approve" Krystal said. "You gone get a chance to meet her tonight at the party." Curtis said. Just then Ashley walked in the room. "

Daddy, mom called she wants you to call her" Ashley said. Curtis rolled his eyes and said "Ok I'll call her later." Ashley walked out "What does she want? Krystal said. "I don't know probably nothing as usual." Curtis said. "Well I'm gone go and help Ashley get dressed and see if mama needs some help; She's making party favors for all the kids" Krystal said. "Party favors. These kids are too old for that." Curtis said. "She thought it would be a good idea to make little bags for them. It's really cute she's putting little things of soap and mouth wash you know little travel size things they can take with them to college. I think they'll like it. She also included a $50 visa gift card in each bag." Krystal said. Curtis shook his head. "She knows she can't afford that."

He said. "Yes she can, Curtis. You pay all of her bills what else has she to do with her money." Krystal said. "I know but I don't want her spending her money like that." He said. "Well she wanted to contribute something. I think it's a good idea." Krystal said. "I guess" Curtis said. Krystal stood up and walked to the door "I'll see you later. Is Marissa coming to the party? "You know she is." Curtis responded. Krystal rolled her eyes and walked out. Curtis picked up the phone and dialed Marissa's home number "Hello" a very sexy voice answered. "Hi Marissa, Ashley told me you wanted to talk to me?" Curtis said. "Well I was wondering if you're...Um friend was coming to the party because I don't think it would be a good idea for us to have our lovers at our daughter's graduation party." Marissa said. "Well I really don't care what you think. I asked her to be here plus she wanted to congratulate Ashley and give her a gift. You can feel free to bring your man if you want to." Curtis said. "Unlike you I have respect for my daughter" Marissa said. Curtis laughed. "That's funny, is there anything else you needed? He said. "Well yes now that you mention it; I'm a little short this month I need some money." She said. "Marissa you get good money from me every month it's more than enough to sustain you until the next month. Why don't you stop trying to live above your means?" Curtis said. Marissa poured on the sweetness she knew she could get Curtis to change his mind. "Your right perhaps I am living above my means but it's hard to get used to living on barely nothing when your use to having it all. I'll try to do better but for now can you give me some money? She said. Curtis sighed "How much? "Well let's see I promised Ashley I would take her shopping to get a whole new wardrobe for college and I have some credit card bills to pay plus we need food so I guess I will need at least ten grand." She said. Curtis almost swallowed his tongue.

He figured she would ask for at least five grand but ten was out of the question. "Are you crazy? You don't need that much money for the few things you named. If that's the case then you're not using the money you get for what it should be used for. And if that's true then I'll be seeing you in court. I'll give you five grand Marissa no more. You better make it last." He said. Marissa smiled to herself she knew that would work. The key with Curtis is to always ask for more than what she needed to get the amount she wanted. "Alright fine I'll try to make it last. Um if you come over later on I'll try and make it worth your while." She said. "Not tonight Marissa. I'll have a check for you tonight at the party. I have to go Marissa bye." He said.

Marissa smiled as she hung up the phone. She had Curtis wrapped around her little finger still. He couldn't resist her even when he tried to. And Miss Lisa was only temporary just like Miss Kristine was; it was only a matter of time before Marissa ran her off. Marissa was planning on wearing something tonight that she knew would drive Curtis crazy and make Lisa mad as hell. Marissa enjoyed interfering in his life it was fun for her because she knew Curtis was not completely over her and she knew she could always draw him to her with sex. She did it to prove a point to Curtis and whomever he was dating to show them that he would always belong to her. Even though she didn't love Curtis and hadn't for a long time she still considered him hers. He was the only man she could control and who she knew loved her completely. He was her ace in the hole; whenever things got bad she knew she could count on him. Marissa looked around her house. It was a very nice house but not as big as Curtis's house and not as elaborate but very nice. Marissa hated it; she felt it was beneath her. All of her friends lived in bigger houses. She hated inviting her men back to her house because she was embarrassed; it was not what she was used to.

The divorce had been hard on Marissa as far as her financial status goes. Even though the money she received each month from Curtis was more than enough for her to take care of the children and herself and then some. Marissa was used to spending unlimited amounts of money whenever she wanted to. This made her mad. She couldn't handle living on a fixed income. Although she had plenty of money in her bank account she wanted more. Marissa barely spent any of the money she'd been getting from Curtis each month because Derek kept money in her pocket not as much as he use to but still it was enough. Lately she had been thinking of ways to get Curtis to buy her a new house. She had asked Derek to buy her a house but he was playing games with her. Marissa really liked Derek but he was seeing her less and less. Marissa knew the signs of a man who was cheating so she always kept her an ace in the hole.

By 8:30 p.m. the party was on and popping. All of Ashley's friends had shown up and they were having a good time on the patio. The DJ was playing the kind of music they liked and they were getting wild. Curtis and Krystal were walking around the party to make sure nobody got out of hand. They were standing by the DJ booth when Lisa walked up to them. Curtis saw her approaching them and he held out his hand to her. She walked up to him and they embraced each other "Hey baby, you look nice" Lisa smiled "Thank you sweetie" Curtis pointed to Krystal and said "I want you to meet my sister Krystal. Krystal this is my girl Lisa." They both shook each other's hands and said in unison "It's nice to meet you" Lisa said, "Curtis has told me so much about you. He's very proud of you." She said. That made Krystal smile. She didn't know how to respond because he hadn't told her anything about Lisa. "That's my big brother." She said. "So how did you two meet? Krystal asked Lisa for lack of anything better to say. "We met at a benefit my company was giving. We were introduced by a mutual friend and we just hit it off." She said. "What company do you work for? "I work at Essence magazine as an editor." Lisa said. Krystal was impressed. Her brother usually went for models and groupies but this woman was not only beautiful but she was smart to. Lisa was a beautiful African American woman. She was about 5'6. She looked like she weighed about 130 pounds if that. She was very slender but shapely; she was Carmel complexion and had long beautiful hair. Krystal wondered if it was all hers. She seemed to be very classy. Krystal and Lisa continued to talk along with Curtis. They found an empty patio table and sat down with a nonalcoholic drink. Curtis was in the middle of telling them about his new gospel rap group when he stopped in mid-sentence. Krystal and Lisa followed his gaze to see what had him so distracted. It was Marissa she walked in looking incredible. Her body was perfect. She was wearing a dress that made all the young boys at the party stop what they were doing just to stare at her.

She was wearing a long black sheer dress that showed her panty and bra or was it her bikini. As she walked toward them she stopped and turned around to speak to one of Ashley's friends and Curtis almost dropped the drink he was holding in his lap. When Marissa turned around he saw that she was wearing the hell out of a thong. That's what had the young boys staring at her. Curtis was practically drooling himself. Krystal just shook her head. She couldn't believe that Marissa would show up to her daughter's graduation party looking like that. What a hoe, Krystal thought to herself. Lisa turned back around and was staring at Curtis. He couldn't take his eyes off of Marissa. Lisa was pissed. Finally Marissa made her way over to the table where they sat. "Hello everybody" Marissa said. She only looked at Curtis when she spoke. She didn't even acknowledge Krystal and Lisa.

Curtis looked at Lisa who was looking at him as if she wanted to kill him. He tried to play it off "Um hi Marissa" again she only spoke to him. Lisa was waiting for Curtis to say something about her rudeness but he never said anything. In fact they were staring in each other's eyes. Lisa cleared her throat and said "Hi Marissa nice to see you again" Marissa cut her eyes for a moment at Lisa and responded "Likewise." Krystal didn't even bother to speak she knew Marissa didn't like her and she didn't care one bit. She just sat back and watched while Miss Thing put on a show. "Where's Ashley? Marissa asked. "She's around here somewhere." Curtis said. "Let me go and see if I can find her. I'll talk to you later" She said. Marissa walked away. Krystal shook her head. Of course she wasn't going to join them that would defeat the purpose of wearing such a seductive outfit. The whole purpose was to get Curtis attention and she couldn't get his attention sitting at the table not while Lisa was there. But then again she wore it for Lisa too, to make her mad. This is going to be an interesting night. Krystal thought to herself. Curtis watched as she walked away. He tried not to but the sight of her in that thong had him mesmerized. Lisa was trying to remain calm. She felt totally disrespected by Curtis. I'm a confident woman and know that I look good but this is some bullshit. How he gon' just stare her hoochie ass down right in front of me. He won't be hitting this tonight. Let him run back to her ass. Lisa thought to herself.

When Curtis was able to refocus on the two women who were sitting with him again; Lisa was pissed she got up from the table and said "Excuse me" she walked away. "Lisa, where you going? Curtis called after her. Lisa turned and said to Curtis "I'm going to the bathroom I'll be right back." Lisa wasn't the kind of woman who got jealous easy but this was too much for her. Her ass wore that sleazy outfit on purpose for one reason only to attract him. I'm a class act and I will not allow that hoe to bring me down to her level. But this Negro will respect me or I'll be gone out of his life so fast his head will spin. Lisa told herself as she walked to the bathroom. She walked passed Marissa as she was speaking with Ashley and her friends. The boys were all crowding around her wanting to be introduced. Marissa smiled as she watched Lisa walk away obviously upset. Her plan was working and she knew she could have Curtis upstairs in the bed right now if she wanted to.

"You know you were wrong" Krystal said to Curtis. "What? Curtis asked. Krystal shook her head and laughed, "Don't even go there. You know what I'm talking about. How could you treat Lisa like that in front of Marissa? Krystal said. "Krystal what are you talking about?" "Curtis stop playing. You know that was disrespectful the way you stared her hoochie mama ass down in front of your girlfriend; you still sleeping with her aint' you?" Krystal said. Curtis took a deep breath and blew it out "That's none of your business Krystal" He said. "Just be honest Curtis" Krystal said. Curtis shook his head "Look I don't have to justify myself to you. So what if I'm still sleeping with her from time to time. She is my wife." He said. "Ex-wife if you've forgotten. But I can see that's the way she wants you to think of her as still being your wife; that way she can still have access to your money" Krystal said. Curtis looked down at his drink; he didn't respond. "Curtis when are you gone stop letting her use you? Why can't you get over her? Is she the best sex you ever had or something?" Krystal asked. Curtis looked up at Krystal "Don't start" He said. Krystal held her hands up and shook her head. "I'm not trying to tell you how to live your life brother but wake up and smell the coffee." She laughed "You know I'm gone pray that God bless you with a woman who'll make you forget all about Marissa." Krystal said. Curtis held his drink up at Krystal and said; "Do that" She laughed and rolled her eyes.

Krystal watched Marissa all night flirting with the young boys and Curtis. Once she was playing with one of the boys and supposedly accidently fell into Curtis's lap. He held on to her a little too long. As a result of that Lisa walked out of the party. Curtis ran behind her to talk to her. She had seen enough and didn't return to the party. Marissa was happy as ever. She had run Lisa off or at least out of the party where she could have full access to Curtis and he allowed it. That man will never learn. Krystal thought to herself. She found herself thinking of Yvette in connection to her brother again. Hmm I wonder. She began thinking that Yvette would be good for Curtis. But naw that wouldn't work she's so hung up on Tony she can't see straight. She thought to herself. Krystal put that out of her mind and enjoyed the rest of the party. Finally it was time for Ashley to open her gifts. She had so many of them there was no way she would be able to open them all. Krystal conducted the opening of the gifts. She gave her only gifts from her mother, grandmother, hers and her Lil brother's to open and a few of her close friends. The rest she could open later.

Ashley received a two thousand dollar check from her aunt Krystal and she received a photo autograph book from her grandmother along with another thousand-dollar check. Marissa got her some expensive cell phone she wanted and she was taking her on a shopping spree before she went away to school. Lil Curtis got her a comforter set and a fifty dollar gift card. Curtis of course gave her the brand new car that everyone saw sitting in the driveway with a big red bow on it. Ashley made out good. She had over five thousand dollars in cash for school and plenty of dorm room items. The party was over at 1 a.m. Krystal made sure all the kids who didn't drive got picked up by their parents. Then she made sure Ashley and her friends who were spending the night had everything they needed. She checked in on Lil Curtis and her mother and then went to her own room. On her way to her room she heard faint sounds of moans. At first she thought she was hearing things but she heard it again. She looked down the hall at Ashley's room and wondered if they were watching a porno or something. She walked a little closer to Ashley's door to see if she could hear it again but all she heard were the girls giggling and laughing and talking.

Krystal walked back toward her room and there it goes again. She knew it wasn't coming from her mother's room and it better not be coming from Lil man's room the only other place it had to be coming from was Curtis's room. Then it dawned on her she hadn't seen Curtis or Marissa since the party ended. Krystal creped down the hall towards Curtis' room. She put her ear to the door and sure enough that's where the sounds were coming from. As she put her ear to the door all she could hear Curtis and Marissa making love. Krystal shook her head and walked away. "Men will do anything for sex" she said out loud.

Chicago

Leonard sat at his dinette table eating his microwave dinner. It was lasagna his favorite. But it didn't taste anything like his wife's lasagna. He missed Yvette something awful. Leonard kept tabs on Yvette. He knew she was living with that goon Tony Riche in Atlanta. He even knew where Tony lived. He knew she and her girlfriends were going into the promotion business. Leonard took regular trips to Atlanta just to keep an eye on Yvette. He still hadn't gotten over her and their divorce. In his sick mind she would always belong to him. He would not allow her to walk out on him. Leonard was very determined and confident that he would have Yvette back one day. It was hard to get to her because Tony had such good security at his house and they always traveled with bodyguards when they were together. He wasn't able to catch her alone yet. That made him mad but he wasn't going to give up trying. One of these days she was going to have his baby.

Leonard continued to frequent strip clubs and have sex with strippers and hookers. He liked sleazy women in the bedroom. He had finally run Denise off. He had beaten her so much she didn't even look the same any more. She couldn't go back to stripping so one day when Leonard wasn't home she took all her clothes and stole some money from him and ran away. Leonard never heard from her again nor did he look for her. He had plenty of women to replace Denise. Leonard pushed the plate away from him. He sat there looking down at the table. He felt like seeing Yvette; Leonard walked over to his computer and sat down in the chair. He went to Yvette's radio website to look at her picture. He did this often when he just couldn't stand it anymore. He masturbated while reminiscing on the many times they made love.

Atlanta August 27th 2007

It was the first concert the Diva Promotions had sponsored. The place was packed. They had the hottest rappers in the industry performing and two of the hottest R&B singers performing along with the rappers. Plus they had planned a hot after party that would rival any of the big Hollywood after parties. It was an exciting night. Krystal, Yvette and Tonya were back stage. They had a few close friends and family members to join them on their big debut night. They all wore white for their promotional pictures. They mingled with their guest before it was time for the show to start. Krystal was the only one who didn't have family there. She said her brother was planning on coming but she hadn't heard from him. Yvette had invited her sisters down for their debut but the only one who could make it was Octavia. Octavia was going to attend the after party and then fly back home at the end of the evening. Yvette wanted her to stay but she had to get back to go to work.

It was getting close to show time so the ladies made their rounds to the stars dressing rooms to make sure they were comfortable and had all they needed. Finally it was curtain time. The ladies were introduced and the crowd was going wild. They walked out on the stage looking fabulous. They had all been in the gym working out together to make sure they looked good for this night. They hired a trainer to get their bodies' fine-tuned and toned up for this big event. A lot was riding on their look that was their reputation. They got the crowd hyped up and had a good time with them before the first act was introduced.

By the end of the concert, their guests back stage were heading out to the after party. The ladies hung around to make sure the stars were paid and to confirm who would be showing up for the after party. Backstage was crowded as ever. Yvette was moving through the crowd to get back to the office when she ran smack dead into a hard wall. It wasn't a wall it was a hard chest; a very muscular chest. As soon as she hit the wall of muscle she felt two very strong arms circle her waist. Immediately she thought it was Tony but it couldn't be Tony he wasn't there because he was overseas. Yvette looked up into two very beautiful hazel eyes. She found herself mesmerized by those eyes. He still held her around the waist. Yvette couldn't stop staring at him she tried to pull herself out of it but it was hard. Say something you idiot. Don't just stand here like a death mute. She was yelling at herself. Finally he spoke "You alright Shorty?" Yvette opened her mouth to speak but nothing came out. Curtis laughed he got this reaction from women all the time. He still held her around her small waist. She felt good in his arms he didn't want to let her go. He remembered her from the night in Las Vegas. She's Tony Riche's woman. He thought to himself. Damn she fine and she smell good…Mmm and nice soft body. Curtis was thinking as he continued to hold Yvette in his arms.

Finally Yvette found her voice "I'm sorry, I…I was just looking for somebody. Please excuse me." She said. She tried to pull away from Curtis but he had a firm hold on her. When she pulled away he resisted and pulled her closer to him. Yvette felt flutters in her stomach. He smelled so good she was about ready to faint in his arms. Yvette couldn't believe this was happening to her again. This time she didn't pull away from him. She was hoping he was going to kiss her. He's so strong and fine. Oh my God I love this man. Yvette told herself. Finally Curtis let her go and held her chin gently in his hand and said "Be careful back here baby. I wouldn't want you to get hurt." He winked at her and walked away.

Yvette stood there looking at him walk away until he got lost in the crowd. She was breathing so fast she had to take a few deep breaths to calm herself down. She composed herself and kept walking through the crowd. When all the business was concluded the ladies headed to the after party. They hired a white limo for the night. Inside the car the ladies toasted their success. "Whew what a night" Tonya said as she sipped her champagne. "Yes, what a night" Yvette said with a smile on her face as she sipped her champagne. "I wish y'all could have met my brother. He popped in and popped right out but at least he showed up." Krystal said. Yvette was on cloud nine she couldn't stop thinking of her encounter with Curtis Abney. The girls would never believe her if she told them but she didn't want to tell them or anybody for that matter it was a very private and special moment for her and she wanted to leave it that way. Yvette knew she would be thinking of this moment when she was home alone bored and feeling unappreciated, unwanted, not special this would help her to carry on when she felt hopeless.

This was a big night for the Divas and they pulled it off. The after party was just as successful as the concert. It was close to 4am when Yvette got home. She climbed the stairs to her bedroom slowly. The house was so quiet and lonely when Tony wasn't home. Rosie lived there too so she knew she wasn't completely alone but Rosie wasn't family. She had no interest in mingling and spending time with her boss. Yvette entered the bedroom and stood in the middle of the floor. Tony was never home it was getting to be a bother. She called his cell phone to see if he would answer. He should be up she thought. His phone was ringing. Yvette sat down on her bed and took her shoes off. His phone was still ringing finally he picked up but all she could hear was a woman's voice in her ear screaming her man's name in a strange accent. Yvette's heart sank to her knees. She could hear the woman constantly screaming and moaning. Then she heard Tony's voice talking to the woman just like he did her when they were making love. He must have tried to hit the ignore button but somehow answered the phone and didn't know it. Yvette threw the phone down and started crying. How could he do that to me? She thought and cried herself to sleep. She never even got undressed.

At 9:30 a.m. the house phone was ringing. It woke Yvette up she got up and looked at the clock. She laid back down trying to ignore the phone. She was in no mood to talk to anybody this morning. Whoever it was kept calling back to back so she picked it up "Hello" "Good morning baby, did I wake you? Tony said. Yvette looked at the phone "This mutherfucka" "Yes you did wake me. So why don't you call back some other time" she said and hung up the phone. Tony called right back and Yvette answered "What" She said. "What the hell is wrong with you? Why did you hang up on me? He said. "I'm sleeping Tony goodbye." She said. Yvette hung up again this time she turned the ringer off. She lay back down but then her cell phone started ringing. She let it ring until she couldn't stand it anymore. She got up out of the bed and walked over to the phone and picked it up and pressed the ignore button then turned it off. Yvette noticed she was still wearing her clothes so she started to undress and put on some pajamas. When she got back in the bed and pulled the covers over her, she heard a knock at the door. "Come in" She said. Rosie walked in "Excuse me but Mr. Riche is on the phone for you. He says it's very important that he speaks with you" Rosie said. "Tell Mr. Riche I don't want to talk to him" Yvette said. Rosie looked a little unsure. She held the phone in her hand. She put it to her ear and said "Um she said she does not want to talk to you" Yvette watched Rosie's face as she listened to Tony. Again she looked unsure as she relayed his message "He said to tell you to get your ass on the phone now" Rosie said. "Tell Tony to kiss my black ass" Yvette said. Rosie frowned and shook her head as if to say, "I can't say that" "Tell him" Yvette yelled. Rosie relayed Yvette's message. She listened and then walked toward Yvette with the phone and handed it to her and walked out of the room. Yvette took a deep breath and let it out.

She picked up the phone and said "What" "Yvette what the hell is going on? Why aren't you answering my calls? Tony yelled. He was pissed he had never spoken to her that way before. But she didn't care she was fed up with his lies and cheating. "Tony I don't wanna talk to you so stop calling me" Yvette said. "I'll call you whenever I want to that's my damn house" Tony said. "Oh so it's like that? "Well how about I just move out of your damn house huh? Yvette said. "Yvette what's wrong with you? Tony asked. "You a dog and I can't stand you" Yvette said. "Baby where's this coming from? Tony said.

Yvette hung up the phone again. She turned the ringer off on that phone and threw it on the floor. She pulled the covers over her head and lay there until she fell asleep. When she woke up it was close to 3:30 p.m. Yvette showered and went downstairs to the kitchen to get some orange juice. She passed Rosie on the steps and Rosie said "Mr. Riche called back and he said for you to call him as soon as you were awake." Rosie told her. Yvette smiled at Rosie and said "I'll get right on that" and she kept walking. She didn't mean to be rude to Rosie but she was mad at Tony. Yvette would apologize to Rosie later. Yvette took her juice and sat on the patio for a few minutes then she went back upstairs to her bedroom and closed the door. It was a beautiful Sunday afternoon and all she wanted to do is curl up and sleep for the rest of her life. Yvette was depressed. She closed the curtains so she couldn't see the sunshine then grabbed her cell phone. She knew Tonya and Krystal had probably been blowing her phone up. When she turned her phone back on the only calls she had missed were from Tony. He left her a thousand text messages as well as voicemails. She read them and put her phone back down. Yvette went back to sleep and didn't awake until 7:30 p.m. she got up and showered and put on a fresh pair of pajamas and went back to bed. She lay in bed watching Lifetime for hours. Finally her cell rang she looked at it expecting to see Tony's number but it was Krystal. She answered, "Hey Krystal, what's up girl? "Hey boo, whatcha doing? "Nothing just lying in the bed watching Lifetime." Yvette sounded sad "You alright? "Yes" "You don't sound alright boo. What's wrong? Yvette couldn't hold it in any longer. She told Krystal the whole story in between sobs. She was so heartbroken. Krystal felt sorry for Yvette. She had been through so much in this last past year and a half.

"Yvette I am so sorry to hear that. I'm even sorrier that you hurting; Yvette why don't you just move out? Krystal said. Yvette continued to cry and sob. "I love him so much. I don't know if I can. I'm so tired of being hurt Krystal. Why am I always the one to get hurt? Why can't anybody ever treat me right? Yvette sobbed. Krystal had heard enough "Sweetheart why can't you treat yourself right? Yes I know you've been hurt and it sucks but stop putting yourself in the position to get hurt. I know we can't help who we fall in love with but we can help how we allow ourselves to be treated. Yvette, Baby, start loving YOU! You deserve so much better. So what a man is taking care of you? So what he got you living in his million-dollar home? All of that means nothing if he doesn't know how to treat you, sweetie. If he's gon' cheat on you and lie to you then it's not worth it; not to mention it's a sin to be living with a man out of wedlock. You've got to wake up honey and start loving you and start loving God. Put God first in your life Yvette.

Honor His word and keep His commandments then and only then will you truly be happy. God will send you the man you need; someone who he has handpicked just for you, someone who'll love you the way you deserve to be loved and treat you like the queen you

34

are. You can't expect a man to treat you with love and respect if he's not treating God with love and respect. If God is not first in his life then he's not worthy of your time. You shouldn't want a man in your life that's not following God. Honey if he can't honor God he'll never honor you." Yvette listened she knew Krystal was right. Ever since she'd left Leonard her relationship with God had not been the same. She got carried away with Tony and fell in love with him. Now here she is a year and a half out of an abusive marriage and she was still hurting emotionally and crying. Yvette felt so weak so ashamed for allowing herself to go right back to the emotional despair she once was in; it was going to be hard to pull herself back this time. But she had to find the strength to do it.

She talked to Krystal a while longer and then ended the call. Yvette didn't want to talk anymore. She lay back down and tried to go back to sleep. It was hard to get Tony off of her mind but finally she was able to sleep. At 10:00 p.m. the phone rang. Yvette looked at the clock next to the bed. She knew it was Tony. She hesitated before picking up the phone. "Hello" "Yvette what the fuck! Tony was yelling in the phone. I've been calling you all night and you not taking my calls? "What's wrong? He yelled "Tony I don't feel like talking right now" Yvette said. "I don't give a damn what you feel like. We gon' get to the bottom of this shit right now." Tony yelled. Yvette started to cry again "Why are you crying Yvette? What's wrong? What did I do? Tony yelled. She was sobbing uncontrollably "Yvette what's wrong? I can't understand you baby calm down." Yvette tried to control her sobs but she was hurt. Tony stopped talking to give her a chance to settle down.

Finally when her sobs ceased he asked very calmly "Baby what is it? "I rather not say Tony," she said. "Why? He asked. She started to cry again "Tony I'm so hurt. How could you do this to me? Yvette cried. "Do what baby? He asked. "I heard you with that woman. I heard you making love to her." Yvette said. Tony's heart sank now he understood. He started to think fast "Baby what woman? He said. You know what I'm talking about Tony. She was calling your name and I heard your voice." Yvette said. "Naw baby, you got this all wrong sweetie. I promise there's been a misunderstanding." Tony said. "No there hasn't" Yvette said. "Baby yes there has." He said.

"No Tony I'm tired of your explanations. You only gon' lie to me again." Yvette said. "I'm not, listen to me baby please" Tony pleaded. "Why should I Tony? What you gon' tell me this time? That I dialed the wrong number, that wasn't your voice I heard?" She said. "Yvette baby that wasn't my voice you heard." Tony said. "Oh really so I dialed your cell phone number. Hear some foreign woman screaming and moaning your name and then I hear your voice and now you want me to believe that it wasn't you?" Yvette said. "It wasn't me" "Then who was it Tony!?" Yvette yelled "Baby calm down" Tony said. "Don't tell me to calm down dammit. Who was it?" She yelled.

"It must have been my body guard. I had to pick up an extra guy when I got here because Ray couldn't make this trip with me so when I got here my manager had hired this guy his name is Tony to." Tony said. "Why the hell did he have your cell phone Tony? Yvette asked. "Baby I'm getting to that part. I had to go and train and I usually give my cell phone to Ray to hold when I'm sparring. I have him answering my calls. Tony was taking his place so I had him holding my phone and answering my calls when I was unavailable. So that's whose voice you heard baby" Tony said. Yvette couldn't believe his stupid answer "Is he black? She asked. "No he was Italian" Tony responded. "Hmm well the man I heard was most definitely a black man and it was your voice I heard because you were saying the same thing you say to me when we fuck" Yvette said. "Baby please believe me it wasn't me. I promise it wasn't me." Tony said.

"I can't explain why his voice sounded like mine but it wasn't me. I was in my room sleep. Tony said. Yvette thought about it; he could be telling the truth. Ray did hold his phone while he sparred with his trainer. Maybe this was all a mistake. Yvette hoped it was she wanted to believe Tony. She was quiet on the phone "Baby say something" He said. "I don't know what to say Tony." Yvette said. "Say you believe me baby. I love you" Tony said. Yvette felt her heart growing softer towards him. "I love you too" She responded. "Then let's stop this fighting. Why don't you come down here and be with me ok boo? I really miss you baby." He said. That sounded like a good idea. Yvette would have to take off work for a few days but she was sure Krystal would allow it. "I'll see if I can" Yvette said. "Good I'll have your airline tickets waiting for you." Tony said. Yvette smiled "I really miss you." She said. "I miss you too baby. I can't wait to see you and make love to you." Tony said. Yvette was feeling all mushy inside. She was definitely going to get to Italy to be with her man. When she finished talking to Tony she called Krystal right up and told her she needed to take a few days off to go to Italy to handle some business with Tony. Krystal reluctantly agreed although she knew Tony would slither his way out of it if he hadn't already.

The next morning Yvette was up early she went and got her hair done and got waxed and purchased a new bikini for her trip. She had really been toning up and looked better than ever and couldn't wait to show off her body to her man. By 2:00 p.m. Yvette was sitting on the airplane in first class waiting for them to takeoff. She couldn't wait to see Tony. It was going to be a long flight but it was going to be worth it to see her man. Yvette slept most of the way there. But finally the long flight came to an end and she was landing in Italy. Yvette exited the terminal looking for her boo. She didn't see him right away but as she walked further she saw him standing next to his limo wearing black sunglasses and talking on his cell phone looking good. Yvette's heart skipped a beat. Tony spotted her moving towards him. He ended his call and walked to meet her. They embraced each other. Tony picked her up off her feet while he hugged her. He put her down and kissed her on the lips. They kissed each other passionately then Tony grabbed her hand and they walked to the limo and got in.

Back in Tony's hotel room it was on and popping, Tony made love to Yvette for hours and she enjoyed every minute of it. Afterward they slept for a few hours and woke up and got dressed for dinner. Italy was beautiful and Yvette felt like she was on top of the world. She was with the love of her life and everything was right. After dinner Tony and Yvette walked hand in hand through the streets of Italy. It was a perfect evening. They strolled together looking in shop windows and talking and kissing. Later that night back in the hotel Tony had Yvette screaming his name; afterward Yvette was laid out on the bed basking in the afterglow of her orgasms. She felt so good, so at peace and so in love she could hardly breathe.

Los Angeles August 2007

Curtis made it home in time to see his daughter off to college. Ashley and her best friend Renee were driving down to Florida together in Ashley's new car. Curtis was worried about the girls driving alone. He wanted to fly them down and have her car shipped to her but they wanted to drive. He made sure they got an early start in the morning so they wouldn't have to be on the road in the dark. Marissa had taken Ashley shopping just like she promised and she had a crap load of new clothes. She was taking most of them with her the rest she left behind at her dad's house. Curtis rented a small U-Haul and had it latched to the back of Ashley's car. It was big enough for both of Ashley and Renee to put their things in.

The girls were so excited about their trip it was their first experience being on their own and they were eager to get going. Curtis, his mother and Lil Curtis said goodbye to Ashley and Renee and they were on their way. Ashley still had to stop at Marissa's house and say goodbye so Curtis let her go after he gave her more money for the road. The rest of her graduation money he had wired to a bank on campus for her to have access to whenever she needed it. Curtis watched her pull away. His heart felt heavy as he watched his baby girl drive away to college. He realized the next time he would see her she would have experienced a lot and she would never be his little girl ever again. Curtis prayed his baby would make it safely to school.

He made Ashley promise to call him when she reached school. Curtis took his mother home after they saw Ashley off. Lil Curtis was going to spend the day with his grandmother so Curtis had some free time on his hands. He and Lisa hadn't spoken much since Ashley's graduation party. She told Curtis she needed some space because she felt like he was still in love with his ex-wife. Curtis tried to argue and tell her he wasn't but she still wanted to take a break. So he let her go. He realized he let Marissa come between him and another girlfriend. Curtis allowed his mind to wander to that night in Atlanta when he had run into that beautiful creature. That soft warm body he held in his arms briefly. He couldn't remember her name but he definitely remembered her pretty face and banging body. She was so sexy and so damn interesting to him. He didn't know why; he had never spent any real time talking to her but she was so alluring. He wondered if she was still with Tony. He didn't remember seeing Tony that night. Curtis promised himself if he ever ran into her again he would spend some time and get to know her. All he could picture was her in his bed. The thought made him aroused. He dialed Lisa's number on his cell. She answered "Hello" "Hey what's up? "Hi Curtis, how are you? "I'm good and yourself? "I can't complain." "I was just in the neighborhood and wondered if I could drop in and see you? "Hmm it's kind of early Curtis" "I know. Do you have company or something?" Lisa laughed. "Is that your way of asking if I am sleeping with somebody else? "Maybe" Curtis said. Lisa sighed. "No Curtis there is no one else." She said. "If there is nobody else then you must not want to see me?" Curtis said. Lisa giggled again "I never said I didn't want to see you." She said. "So what's up? You gone let me keep circling your block or are you gone let me come up?" Curtis said. "Well first of all I didn't know you were circling my block and secondly you should have called first before driving all the way over here." Lisa said playfully. "Well like I said I was in the neighborhood so it's not like it's an inconvenience." Lisa looked out her balcony window to see if she could see Curtis's car. Lisa lived on the 6th floor of the Regatta Seaside Condominiums in Marina Del Rey. She saw Curtis parked in front of her building. "I guess since you were in the neighborhood you can come on up. But don't make this a habit" Lisa joked.

Lisa opened the door when she heard Curtis getting off the elevator. She had already showered after her workout this morning so she was fresh, hot and ready for Curtis. She was no fool she knew what he wanted and she didn't mind because she wanted the same thing. Curtis walked in and walked right up to Lisa. He wrapped his arms gently around her waist and pulled her to him and kissed her. Lisa broke the kiss and said "Well good morning" she smiled as she looked up at Curtis who was still holding her. "Good morning" Curtis said seductively. He bent his head and kissed her again then he lifted her off her feet and kicked the door closed with is foot and carried her to the bedroom. Curtis hadn't realized until now how much he missed Lisa. Curtis and Lisa made love and spent the rest of the day together. Curtis enjoyed Lisa's company but he couldn't help thinking back to that lovely woman. Curtis began to wonder about her; what she liked, what she disliked, no woman had ever had this kind of an effect on him. Not even Marissa; she was just different in a way he couldn't explain. He didn't know her to even know she was different but it just seemed like she was. Curtis was very attracted to her. He looked over at Lisa; she was chatting away about something at work. He tried to tune in and pay attention but his mind kept wandering to that woman. He saw himself with her walking on the beach holding hands and laughing. Curtis shook his head to clear that vision from his mind. He felt like a wimp; he was acting like a woman. Curtis looked at Lisa again attempting to pay attention. The more he listened to her he realized he was no longer interested in her. She was a nice woman and even beautiful but his interest for her just wasn't there anymore. It didn't make sense to him because just this morning he had realized that he missed her. Maybe it was just the sex I missed, Curtis thought to himself. Curtis found himself at a crossroad. He was divorced and dating and up until a week ago he was happy or at least satisfied with his life and the way things were going. But since he had made that trip to Atlanta and bumped into that woman he just wasn't satisfied with his life anymore. His life to him seemed boring like it was lacking something. When Curtis left Lisa that evening he knew he wouldn't be seeing her anymore.

Curtis was going back out on the road in a few days. He was going to take his son with him to Chicago then bring him back home for school. It was his turn to take Lil' man for six months as part of the divorce. Curtis had some things to wrap up at the studio before he left for the road. They were scheduled to be in Chicago in two days and from there they were heading to Detroit then New York City from New York they were going to Minnesota and finally the last stop was Miami Florida. Curtis wouldn't be able to join them in all of the states because his son had to go to school. But he had the right people in place to take care of things when he couldn't be there. He did plan to join them in Miami Florida so he could check in on Ashley. The whole tour was scheduled to last about a month and a half. As Curtis was packing his house phone rang "Hello" It was Jonathan Curtis's best friend and business partner. "Hey what's up man? You all ready to leave? Jonathan said. "Naw not yet but I'm getting it together." "Damn man, why do you sound so gloomy?"

Jonathan said. "What do you mean? I'm fine." "You don't sound fine. What's up man?" "Nothing, it's just. Nothing man it's nothing. So we got everything squared away for this trip?" Curtis asked. "Yep, all the plane tickets will be waiting for us at the airport and I just spoke to both of the group's managers and they are all set and ready to go. So we good!" "Alright, good looking." "So what are you doing tonight? Jonathan asked. "Um... nutin' why? "Well Mary is throwing this little get together tonight for her job at the house. You know it's a meet and greet for her new employees and she wanted me to ask you if you wanted to come." "Uh oh, I smell trouble. Who is she?" Curtis said. "Who is who? Jonathan asked. "Don't play with me Jonathan. Who is the woman your wife is trying to hook me up with?" Curtis asked. "Aw man, it's not like that." Jonathan said. "Ok it probably is like that, but I don't know she didn't tell me who it was this time. She just asked me to invite you so I'm inviting you. Are you coming?" He said. "Jonathan man I'm not in the mood for one of Mary's 'Find Curtis a woman nights' I just don't feel up to it." Curtis said.

Mary was listening in on the phone and she cut in saying "Curtis, you know I love you and I promise you'll enjoy yourself tonight. Come on, you are about to go out on the road and it'll be nice to cut loose one night before you do all that traveling. I'm not asking you to marry her just meet her; how bad can that be?" Mary said. Curtis loved Mary like a sister and had a hard time saying no to her just like he did with his own sister. Curtis sighed. "Fine, I'll come. You know I'm only doing this for you right? I'm not looking for a girlfriend right now." Curtis said. "I know boo, now get your butt over here." Mary said. "I'll see y'all in about an hour." Curtis said.

An hour and a half later Curtis was walking through Jonathan's front door. It looked like the party was jumping. Jonathan saw him walk in and came right over to him. "Glad you could make it man, here" Jonathan handed Curtis a cocktail. Curtis accepted it. It was his usual Patron and cranberry juice. "So where is she?" Jonathan laughed "I believe she's out on the patio with the rest of the women." Curtis looked around the room; there were a few women here and there but most of them were out on the patio. Jonathan and Curtis grabbed a seat at the bar. Jonathan introduced Curtis to some

41

of Mary's co-workers. Mary worked for Universal Studios in Hollywood so most of her co-workers were directors and writers. Curtis and Jonathan mingled with the men and were having a pretty good time when Mary came in off the patio and spotted who she was looking for. Mary strutted over to Curtis and slipped her arm through his. "Hey stranger" Curtis turned towards Mary and hugged her "Hey" "So you gon' hide in here all night or are you going to join us on the patio?" She was referring to Curtis and Jonathan. They both looked at each other and rolled their eyes. Mary grabbed Jonathan's arm and walked both Curtis and her husband out on the patio. When they stepped out on the patio Curtis noticed Mary had tables set up for people to sit and eat and talk.

She led them to a table full of women. Curtis surveyed the women around the table trying to pick out the ugliest one. She would most likely be the one Mary wanted him to meet. As he looked around most of the women were pretty good looking. Others were average but none he would describe as ugly, which made him feel better. As they reached the table Mary introduced Curtis to all of the women. "It's nice to meet you ladies" Curtis responded. Once the meet and greets were all finished Mary walked them to the next table where only three women sat. Oh shit. Curtis thought to himself. She introduced him to the three women. Again none of the three were ugly in fact they were all very beautiful. Curtis felt his spirits lifting. He was hoping one of them was the woman Mary intended for him to meet. But no such luck it appeared the woman he was intended to meet had not arrived yet. So Curtis and Jonathan found an empty table after making the acquaintance of all the women on the patio and sat down with their drinks.

The gentlemen they were talking to before joined them at the table and again they got into a very interesting conversation about sports, money and women. Curtis was on his third drink and feeling very good when Mary appeared at his side along with a young woman. "Sorry to interrupt you boys but Curtis can I see you for a moment?" Curtis looked up at Mary, he nodded his head yes and took one last swig of his drink and got up. He heard the other guys commenting as he stepped to the side with Mary and the young woman "There she go trying to make another love connection" Mary turned around and said "I heard that Ted. Just remember the last love connection I made you ended up married." Ted looked salty as Mary continued on her business with Curtis. "Curtis I wanted you to meet my good friend Pam. Pam this is Curtis. Pam works on the advertisement team at Universal Studios.

She's been with the company, what six months now, so of course she's new in town so I thought it would be nice if you two met. Curtis is a native here and knows all of the fun places to eat and shop in LA." Curtis looked at Pam she was definitely not ugly. She was very pretty with long hair past her shoulders and light skinned. She looked like she may be from the islands. Curtis was very pleased with what he saw. Mary left them alone. Curtis found an empty table and asked Pam to join him. She already had a drink in her hand but he asked, "Can I get you something? Perhaps another drink or something to eat?" "Oh no, I'm good but thanks for asking." "So you were born and raised here in LA huh?" "Yes, that's right" "And you were the lead singer of the Oakland Boys right?" Curtis smiled "So you recognize me? "Yes of course. I was a huge fan of the Oakland Boys, I still am." Curtis frowned a little "You look too young to even know the music." Pam smiled "I had older sisters who loved your group. They played your albums all the time. I'm not that young." "How old are you? If you don't mind me asking?" "No I don't mind and I'm twenty eight." Curtis was used to dating young women so her age didn't bother him. She seemed to be a nice young woman. They sat and talked for hours. Before he knew it the party was over and people were leaving.

Curtis found Pam to be very interesting. They exchanged numbers and Curtis promised when he got back in town he would take her out. He walked her to her car and said goodnight. Pam got in her car and drove away. Mary walked up behind Curtis and linked her arm in his and said "See now that wasn't so bad was it?" Curtis looked down at Mary and responded with a smile "No it wasn't." "It looks like you two hit it off" Mary said as Curtis shook his head and said playfully "You just gotta know don't you?" Mary smiled and said "I gots to know" "Yes we hit it off if that's what you want to call it." "Uh huh, and did I see you two exchange numbers?" "You gotta know all the business huh? "That's right. Give it up big daddy" "Yes we exchanged numbers Mary, damn" Curtis said. Jonathan walked up "Hey man can you get your nosey wife? Curtis joked "Nosey" Mary hit Curtis playfully on the arm. "One of these days you gon' appreciate my match making skills buddy." "Whatever" Curtis said as Mary walked away. "It looked like you had a good time tonight my brother." Curtis smiled "It was alright" They slapped hands and said goodnight and Curtis got in his car and headed home.

The more things change the more they stay the same

The tongue that brings healing is a tree of life, but a deceitful tongue crushes the spirit. (scripture reference)

December 10, 2007

Yvette put the last of the ornaments on the Christmas tree. She was so excited her whole family was coming for Christmas and Tony had invited his mother and his sister and brother and his family. It was going to be great. Yvette had been with Tony for over two years now and he had never bothered to introduce her to his family. She knew he was born in Barbados and came to Atlanta when he was nineteen to start his fighting career. She knew his mother's name was Eva Riche but that was about it. Tony didn't talk about his family a lot. In fact he never really mentioned anything personal to her. Yvette was hoping this Holiday would bring them closer together and make him want to open up to her and share his world. Since August when Yvette had joined him in Italy she'd found out the woman she heard screaming her man's name in the phone was a woman he had been messing around with for months. But she forgave him for it just like she had his many other indiscretions. Tony still confessed that he loved her on a regular basis but when he was home he was always distracted and cranky.

Whenever she would bring up the subject of leaving he would beg her to stay saying he loved her. Yvette held her hand to the bottom of her stomach. She'd found out two days ago that she was pregnant. She was elated and hoped Tony would be to. She hadn't told him yet because she was trying to save it as a surprise for Christmas. She was a month and a half pregnant. Morning sickness was just starting to set in but Yvette didn't mind it. Tony wasn't around much too even notice her sickness. He was due home today so she wa
s trying to make sure everything would be pretty and festive for him. She was trying to create a "homey" feeling hoping it would make him want to stick around instead of running the streets and traveling all the time.

As far as Diva's Promotions everything was moving along splendidly. They were always busy with parties and concerts and openings. The ladies had been discussing leaving radio to start their business full time in the New Year. They had made many business connections and things were looking good for them. Lately they were trying to come up with new marketing strategies to enhance their business. Yvette was kind of worried about how her pregnancy would affect the business. When Tony finds out she was pregnant he would insist that she would take it easy. Although Yvette wanted the baby she also didn't want to slow down. She enjoyed her work. Yvette looked around everything looked beautiful. She looked at her watch Tony would be home any minute now. She placed her hand on her stomach; it was feeling a little queasy. Yvette hadn't eaten all day so she went into the kitchen to find something she could put on her stomach.

She really didn't have an appetite so she just grabbed some saltine crackers and water. She sat down at the table to eat her snack and didn't realize how tired she was. As she ate the crackers her eyelids started to get heavy. She finished the crackers and walked upstairs to lie down before Tony got home. Before she knew it she had dozed off to sleep; an hour later Tony entered their bedroom with his bags. He looked at Yvette lying there looking beautiful. Tony was relieved to find her asleep because he was supposed to have been home over an hour ago when his plane landed. He had to drop off Tamika, the young woman who accompanied him on his trip. He'd planned to just drop her off and keep going but she got frisky with him in the back of the limo and he had to go upstairs to her apartment with her and finish what they'd started. He showered before he left her place to make sure her scent wasn't on him. Tony loved Yvette but he was bored with their relationship.

He wanted Yvette to be his main woman. He liked having her to come home to but he just couldn't be faithful. He had too much money and too many choices for that. But one day he was planning on marrying her. Tony knew he had been cranky a lot lately with her but he couldn't stand all the questions she would have for him. Did she really think he would be faithful to her? She had to expect this she came from a marriage where her husband did this all the time. He got so mad at Yvette because he was used to doing what he wanted with whom he wanted and not being questioned about it. But he had never taken any of the women he messed with as his main woman like he had Yvette. It was to be expected but he still didn't like it. Tony wanted to kiss her but he was afraid to wake her so he let her sleep. He took his bags to his closet and changed into his lounging pants and lay down next to Yvette and fell asleep.

Yvette woke up hours later to find the room dark and Tony's side of the bed empty. She looked at the clock and couldn't believe she had slept five hours. Yvette jumped up and ran to the closet to see if Tony had been home. She was relieved to find his bags in the closet. He must be downstairs or something.

She went into the bathroom and brushed her teeth and washed her face and freshened up before going down stairs looking for him. When she was confident that she looked beautiful she walked down the stairs in search of her man. She found Tony stretched out in the family room on the phone. It had gotten so that whenever she walked up on Tony while he was on the phone she would stand back and listen before entering the room just to make sure he wasn't talking to a woman; from the sound of it that's exactly what he was doing. "Yeah baby, we can see each other later on tonight" "I can't stay out though, I got to come home to wifey" He said. "Yes I love the way you put it on me baby but I got a woman and she's in first place" Tony said. Yvette heard enough; she tried to swallow the knot that was in the back of her throat. Tears were welling up in her eyes. She shook her head wondering why after all this time whenever she caught him with another woman she wanted to cry. "I should be used to this by now" She told herself. She swallowed hard and dried her eyes and walked into the family room. Tony noticed her immediately and shut up.

Yvette walked towards him with a nervous smile on her face. She was trying to keep from crying but she couldn't keep her face straight. Her eyes were starting to water again. Tony hurried and ended the call pretending to be talking to his manager. Yvette sat down on the love seat next to the chair he was sitting in. Tony put the phone down and said "Hey sleepy head. I was wondering when you was gone wake up." He got up and walked toward her. Yvette held her head down as he approached her trying to compose herself. Tony lifted her chin and was leaning in for a kiss when he noticed her eyes were watery. "What's wrong baby? He said. Yvette tried to play it off and say "Nothing...I nothing" Tony looked into her eyes again and he knew instantly that she had overheard him on the phone. He cursed himself for not being more careful. He didn't mean to hurt her all the time but he felt it was too late to change and besides he didn't want to. He planned to marry her so that should make up for all the pain he was causing her. It had gotten to the point that he didn't even bother to deny it anymore. It was an unspoken confession.

He sat down next to her and pulled her into his arms and hugged her. Yvette couldn't hold back the tears any longer she cried in his arms. Tony felt bad but what could he do? Yvette started to feel queasy again so she moved away from Tony and started to get up to go to the bathroom. Tony watched her go in the bathroom and shut the door. He took a deep breath and let it out and waited for her to return. He heard Yvette gagging in the bathroom and jumped up and ran to the door "Baby are you ok? He yelled. She didn't answer him but kept gagging and throwing up. Tony kept knocking on the door but Yvette wouldn't answer him. He stopped knocking when she stopped gagging and throwing up. He heard her open the mouth wash start gargling and few minutes later she walked out of the bathroom bent over holding her stomach.

Tony looked at Yvette with concern on his face. He held her around her waist and helped her to the couch. "Baby, are you sick?" Tony said. Yvette looked at Tony she wanted to keep her pregnancy a secret but in light of what she just heard she wanted to tell him hoping it would stop him from cheating on her. "Tony I'm pregnant" Yvette said. Tony looked at Yvette in shocked. He smiled "Baby, are you serious? Yvette shook her head yes. "We gon' have a baby?" He said. "Yes" Yvette responded. Tony hugged Yvette and kissed her. "Are you ok? Do you want anything? Come on let me take you upstairs to lie down." He said. Tony scooped Yvette up in his arms and carried her upstairs to their bedroom. He laid her on the bed gently. "How do you feel? Are you in pain or anything? Oh my God? We gon' have a baby." He said. Yvette couldn't help from smiling

Tony was excited just like she hoped he would be. Tony sat down beside Yvette on the bed "Baby I'm so happy and I promise you won't have to worry about me and any other woman ever again. I love you and I'm gon' make you happy." Tony said. Yvette's heart skipped a beat; she really needed to hear that from him. Tony spent the rest of the evening catering to her. Yvette felt so special and so loved by him. She was happy.

December 20th 2007 6:00 p.m.

Yvette was making sure the last details for her Christmas party was taken care of. She consulted with the caterer and the DJ to insure everything was perfect. The caterer came with a serving staff and she made sure everyone knew what she expected of them. She had given Rosie the night off. The house was beautiful and festive looking for the party. They were expecting over a hundred guests to attend the party. Tony had his friends and a few relatives coming and Yvette had invited all of her friends from the station and other business associates Diva Promotions had made. Krystal and Tonya were there helping her take care of the last minute details.

Yvette had told them she was pregnant last week and instead of them being disappointed in her like she had expected they were being very supportive and over protective of her as much as Tony was. Yvette didn't mind she liked the attention. "Yvette I think we have everything together down here sweetie. Why don't you go upstairs and put your feet up for about an hour before you get dressed." Yvette looked at Krystal; she wanted to make sure everything was perfect. She didn't want to embarrass Tony in front of his friends by having things out of order. "I'm ok, I just wanna make sure everything is set" Yvette responded. "Girl take your ass upstairs and sit down" Tonya responded "We got this" Yvette laughed "Alright" "Go on get out of here." Tonya said. When Yvette was out of ear shot she said "That girl is gone lose that baby if she don't slow down." Tonya said. "Tonya don't say that. She's gonna be fine. We'll see to that." Krystal said. "Yes we will" Tonya replied.

They finished up the last details and went upstairs to get dressed for the party. Krystal knocked on Yvette's bedroom door before she went to the guest room. Knock, Knock "Come in" Yvette answered. She was curled up in Tony's lap in a chair in their room. Krystal opened the door and looked surprised because she thought she was interrupting "Oh I'm sorry sweetie. I'll come back later" "No it's alright" Yvette said. "I didn't mean to intrude I just wanted to let you know everything is ready and me and Tonya were going to get dressed. I just wanted to see if you needed anything?" Krystal said. Yvette sat up "No I'm fine. You and Tonya go ahead and get dressed." Yvette said. Krystal nodded her head and turned to leave when Yvette called her name "Krystal, I just wanted to say thank you for all your help and support" She said. Krystal smiled "It ain't nothing. You know I would do anything to help you." She blew Yvette a kiss and cut her eyes at Tony before walking out. He knew Krystal didn't like him. Tony looked at Krystal in a nonchalant way. He didn't have anything against Krystal but he knew she hated the way he treated Yvette and he couldn't blame her. At least he knew she cared about Yvette. Tony held his head down.

He was ashamed of the way he had treated Yvette that's why he planned to propose to her later on during the party. Maybe then Krystal would forgive him. Tony kissed Yvette on the forehead and picked her up. He placed her on the bed and kissed her again "Ima finish getting ready ok boo? Yvette smiled and nodded her head. "I need to go and get ready myself." She said. Yvette moved to get off the bed but Tony stopped her "No you don't. You lie down and get some rest. You've been working so hard getting this party together. It's ok if you rest and make a late appearance at the party" He said. Yvette sat back down and put her feet up on the bed and answered "Yes doctor" Tony winked at her and said, "That's right and don't you forget it. I want my son to be healthy and strong!" He said. "Or your daughter" Yvette responded, "Naw, I can tell it's a boy" "How can you tell that? Yvette asked. "I just feel it." Tony said. Yvette shook her head and smiled as Tony walked back in his closet and finished getting dressed.

By 8:00 p.m. everyone had just about arrived. Yvette was dressed and ready to head downstairs. She was wearing a beautiful gold sequence strapless shirt with gold silk fitted pants to match. She was also wearing her yellow diamond gold necklace and bracelet Tony bought for her. Her shoes were gold open toed shoes with the same yellow diamonds in them to match her jewelry. She wore her hair straight and pulled over to the side. Yvette looked stunning as she walked down the stairs making her entrance as Tony suggested. Krystal and Tonya were the first ones to notice her. They walked up the stairs to meet her and escort her down so she wouldn't trip in her heels. As they descended the stairs Yvette made her rounds greeting all her guests with Krystal and Tonya by her side. As she walked through the party she was scanning the room for Tony wondering why he wasn't the one to escort her down the stairs. It was a big house so it took her a minute to get through the crowd and mingle and take pictures with everybody. Finally she spotted Tony in the corner talking to some woman and standing way to close for her comfort. She looked at Krystal and Krystal said, "Go handle your business. We got yo back." Tonya and Krystal stood back and watched as Yvette approached Tony and the smiling female he was talking to.

Yvette walked up on the side of Tony and linked her arm in his and smiled at him. Tony turned and looked down at Yvette and said "Hey baby" I didn't know you were ready to come down. You should have had somebody to come and get me." He said. You should have come and checked on me yourself. Yvette thought sarcastically to herself. Yvette smiled up at Tony and kissed him tenderly on the lips. Tony returned her kiss and kissed her again. Tamika was getting mad that Tony was disrespecting her; she didn't care that Yvette was his woman, she wasn't his wife so as far as she was concerned Tony was fair game and she did intend on having him. Tamika cleared her throat to remind them she was still standing there. Tony broke the kiss but didn't break his eye contact with Yvette. He looked down and said "You look beautiful baby as always" He kissed her on the cheek. Yvette said "Tony don't be rude introduce us" Tony reluctantly turned towards Tamika. "Baby this Tamika, she's here with Ray and his friends" Tamika gave Tony the evil eye; she didn't appreciate him treating her. "It's very nice to meet you Tamika" Tamika smiled a very phony smile and said "Nice to meet you too" Her sarcasm didn't escape Yvette but she played it off as if she didn't notice.

"Sweetie we have some rounds to make" Yvette said to Tony. "I hope you enjoy the party," Yvette said to Tamika before she and Tony strolled away. Tamika watched Tony lead his woman away with his arm around her waist not even bothering to look back at her. Tamika was furious. She knew about Yvette; Tony made it very clear that she was his number one girl. She didn't expect her to be so pretty and the way he was hanging all over her it was clear to see he really did love this woman. Usually guys who say they have a woman don't pay that much attention to them. She could see she underestimated their relationship and it was going to be a lot more difficult than she thought to come between them. Yvette was in the spot she wanted to be in and since she wasn't wearing a wedding ring she was only a small problem as far as Tamika was concerned. That necklace she was wearing and her bracelet and shoes. That bitch don't deserve all this if she did he wouldn't be in my bed. Tamika told herself. Tamika watched as they stopped and talked to their guest like they were man and wife and everybody treating her like she was his wife. Tamika was from the school of hard knocks and knew how to get what she wanted. She looked around the beautiful mansion soon this would all be hers. When she spoke to Tony later she was going to rip him a new one for ignoring her. I'm the other woman. I should be the one he's looking at with lust in his eyes. Tamika thought to herself.

Tonya and Krystal watched Tamika watching Tony and Yvette and they knew without a shadow of a doubt that she wasn't Ray's guest she was Tony's guest. "She a bold lil' old thang ain't she? Tonya said to Krystal. "That she is but she better watch herself" Krystal responded. They mingled with their colleagues and business associates while keeping an eye on Miss Thang. Tony stuck close to Yvette all-night; doting on her and kissing on her. It drove Tamika crazy. Since Yvette entered the room he had hardly given her a second thought. Yvette had finally broken away from Tony and got with Tonya and Krystal. They talked and laughed for a while. Yvette was there girl so they had to give her the 411 on that Tamika chick. "Look here Yvette I don't know who that woman is" Tonya pointed at Tamika "But you better watch her. It looks like she has a plan for your man. She's been watching y'all all night shooting daggers your way." Yvette looked at Tamika "Yeah I figured as much. She pretty much rolled her eyes when Tony introduced me as his woman." "Well we got your back up in here" Krystal responded "That's for sure" Tonya stated. Yvette slapped hands with her girls "Good looking out, Divas." She said.

Tony walked up and wrapped his arms around Yvette's waist pulling her close to his chest and kissing her on the neck. "I'm sorry to interrupt you ladies but baby I need you to come with me for a second" He said. Yvette looked at Tony suspiciously but followed him. She looked back at her girls and shrugged her shoulders as if to indicate she didn't know what this was about. Tony moved through the crowd towards the DJ stage that was built towards the back of the room. He had a chair sitting on the stage. Tony escorted Yvette up the three stairs to the stage and told her to sit in the chair. Yvette sat down wondering what this was all about. She figured Tony was going to announce to the party that she was expecting his child in October of 2008. That made her kind of nervous because she wasn't ready to tell everybody yet. She tried to smile and hide her nervousness.

Yvette was sitting on the stage for everyone in the party to see her. The DJ handed Tony the microphone. "Good evening everybody. I hope everybody is enjoying themselves. My beautiful woman up here worked hard to pull this party off and I want to say she did a splendid job in doing so." He said. The crowd clapped in agreement. He looked at Yvette and said "She's good at pulling things together at the last minute under pressure. And that's what I love about her. She's the strongest woman I know. She's also beautiful and incredibly sweet." He said. Yvette was so touched by the things Tony was saying. He did appreciate her and that made her happy more than anything. Tony stared into Yvette's eyes and said "That's why" He began to kneel on one knee "I want her to be wife" Yvette was shocked; she put her hands over her mouth.

The crowd started clapping as Tony pulled out a mid-size black box with a gold bow on it and said to Yvette "Baby, I know I haven't been the best lately and I know I've put you through a lot over these past two years but if you will allow me to I plan on spending the rest of my life making it up to." Tony opened the box and said "Yvette will you marry me baby? Tears were streaming down Yvette's face. The crowd was silent awaiting her answer. She looked down at the beautiful Ross Simon 10 carat white gold diamond ring. Yvette looked back up at Tony and hugged him. "Does that mean yes baby?" Tony said into the microphone. Yvette was crying and laughing at the same time "Yes" Tony picked Yvette up and hugged her so tight. The crowd erupted with applause, whistles and shouts. Krystal and Tonya had made their way to the front of the DJ booth

PURPOSE IN THE PAIN

to congratulate their girl. Tony hugged and kissed Yvette for a while then he set her back on her feet. He put the microphone up to his mouth and said "This morning my beautiful bride to be surprised me in telling me that I'm going to be a father in October" the crowd exploded again with applause. Tony lied because he didn't want people to think he was only marrying Yvette because she was pregnant which, was the truth but he didn't want the press to have a field day with it.

Krystal and Tonya rushed forward as Tony helped Yvette off of the stage. They both hugged her at the same time. They all had tears in their eyes. People had crowded around them trying to congratulate them. Tamika sat in the back of the room with tears in her eyes out of anger. That bastard could have told me he was gone pop the question tonight. She told herself. She felt so stupid. Here she thought she was going to be able to take Tony from Yvette and now he's marrying her. She walked over to Ray and told him she was ready to go. Ray blew her off he was waiting around with the rest of his crew to congratulate Tony. Tamika walked away pissed she went and sat in the corner and watched Tony and Yvette. Yvette was elated she had so many people around her hugging her and congratulating her. When most of the crowd had a chance to congratulate them she was able to talk with Krystal and Tonya again. They held her hand looking at her ring. It was a beauty "Tony really went all out on this rock" Tonya stated. "I know right" Yvette responded. "I can't believe he asked me to marry him" Yvette was so happy. Krystal was happy for her too but she couldn't help but feel a little uneasy about it; she didn't think Tony was the man that God had for Yvette but she didn't want to tell her that because she didn't want to spoil her moment.

The photographer came forward to take pictures of Tony and Yvette. They posed for pictures together then she had Tonya and Krystal to join in. Yvette made sure she got pictures with all of her important guests and friends. Finally the night came to an end. Yvette and Tony said goodnight to all of their guests. Yvette went upstairs with her girls so they could get their overnight bags. Tony spotted Tamika still sitting in the corner looking salty. He looked behind him to make sure Yvette was gone then he approached her. "Hey what's up, you didn't catch a ride with Ray? He said. Tamika gave Tony a dirty look "I didn't wanna catch a ride with Ray. You taking me home" Tamika said. Tony frowned and laughed "You better get yo ass up and go grab a ride with Ray" He said. Tamika stood up and got in Tony's face "No, You taking me home. You the one who had me coming here on some bullshit so you'll be the one taking me home tonight" She demanded. Tony was starting to get mad. He moved in closer to Tamika and said. "Look dammit I'm not gone tell you this again; go find Ray. Cus if you mess things up between me and my fiancé I'm gone whip your ass" Tony grabbed Tamika up by her shirt and pushed her to the door.

The cleaning crew looked up but tried not to pay attention to them. Tamika shoved Tony's hands off of her and pointed her finger in his face "Look Tony I was trying to tell you this in a subtle way that's why I wanted you to take me home tonight; but since you wanna get ignorant with me then I'll go ahead and tell you right here. I'm pregnant" Tamika said. Tony laughed "Get the hell out of here Tamika" He said. "It's the truth Tony!" She said. "Well it ain't my baby. The only woman I got pregnant is my fiancée so you can get out of here with that" Tony said. "Oh how do you know it's your baby? You've been laid up in my bed for months now so how do you know she wasn't dipping out on you while you were dipping out on her? And why don't you stop with this fiancé talk you just proposed tonight" She said. "Look you little tramp get yo ass out of my house right now!" Tony said. "I'm not going anywhere until we discuss what we gone do about our baby. If you not prepared to do the right thing then Ima have to let your fiancé know she's not the only one pregnant" Tamika said. Tony slapped Tamika across her face. Tamika held her face in disbelief. Then she balled her fist up and started hitting Tony's chest and his arms wherever she could land a blow. She was yelling and screaming "Don't you ever put your hands on me again Tony. I'll have your ass arrested. This ain't over you can believe that" Tamika shouted.

By now Yvette and the girls heard the commotion and were coming down stairs to see what was going on. They stood mid-way on the stairs watching the security throw Tamika out. She was yanking and pulling away from them as they were trying to escort her out in a dignified manner. Tamika looked up and saw Yvette standing on the stairs and she really put on a show "I hope you know you ain't the only one who's pregnant. Ask your man where he was last night. He wanna deny this baby then Ima sue his ass and take him to court for child support. You think you all that cuz you got him to put a ring on your finger. Well you ain't cuz he'll be back in my bed you watch what I tell you. He can't deny this. Ain't that right Tony?" Tony was standing there looking furious at Tamika. He wanted to slap her again but there were too many witnesses. He was afraid to look up at Yvette and see the look in her eyes. This was supposed to be her night and this little bust down destroyed it. Finally she was out of the house but outside she was still yelling and cussing. Some of their guests were still outside getting into their cars. Tony was so embarrassed he didn't know what to do. He was sure Yvette was embarrassed too in front of her two best friends.

Tony finally looked up at Yvette. She looked pale in the face and she was holding the bottom of her stomach. Fear hit Tony as he raced up the stairs to get to Yvette. "Baby, you ok?" He said as he raced up the stairs towards her. Yvette didn't say anything her stomach was starting to cramp and she just wanted to sit down. Yvette's legs had given out which is why she sank down on the stairs. Tony caught her before she hit the stairs and carried her upstairs to the bedroom. Krystal and Tonya raced up the stairs behind him. They all entered the bedroom. Krystal raced forward and pulled the covers back before Tony laid Yvette down. Tonya had ran into the bathroom and got a wet rag to place on her forehead. Tony was on the phone calling the doctor. Krystal sat down next to her "You ok sweetie? Yvette felt weak and tired as she was dozing in and out. The last thing she heard before she closed her eyes was Tony yelling in fear "Baby" "baby hold on the doctor is on his way"

Yvette woke up about forty minutes later to the doctor touching all over her. She looked at him "What happened?" She said. The doctor looked at Yvette and said "You're fine Yvette you were just exhausted that's all. Tell me Yvette what did you have to eat tonight? Yvette thought about it and responded. "Nothing" The doctor nodded and said "And what about earlier today? What did you eat? The doctor asked. Yvette thought again "I had some crackers and water this morning; my stomach was queasy and then again later in the afternoon but that was all I had. I was so busy and I didn't have an appetite." Yvette said. The doctor nodded his head "Yvette what happened to you tonight was due to exhaustion and of course not enough to eat. You're pregnant which means your baby is consuming most of everything you eat. The crackers you ate today gave the fetus a little nourishment but left you depleted. You have to take care of yourself Yvette. You have to have energy and strength to get through the day. If you skip meals like this again the same thing is going to happen and that's not good. Even if you feel like you can't eat anything keep eating the crackers and drinking water or milk or juice if you can stand it. But make sure you are eating." He said. Yvette nodded "I understand"

Tony stepped forward and said. "Don't worry about it Doc I'll make sure she's eating right from now on." Krystal and Tonya were standing around the bed. Yvette looked at both of them and almost burst out laughing; they looked so serious and scared. "What's wrong? Why y'all look so scared? "Girl you scared the shit out of us" Tonya stated. Krystal shook her head in agreement. "I'm sorry I didn't mean to worry anybody but I don't even know what happen all I remember is feeling like my stomach was hurting then I got weak and tired all of a sudden and the next thing I remember is waking up." The doctor spoke up "Listen Yvette even if you have to force yourself to eat you must eat. When it comes time to give birth you won't have the strength to go through it if you keep this up. I want you to come and see me in two days for a follow up visit." He said. The doctor wrote the date and time for her to come into his office. He spoke with Tony for a moment then left.

Tonya and Krystal helped Yvette undress and get into her night-clothes. When Tony came back into the room Yvette was all tucked away in bed. Krystal and Tonya kissed Yvette on the cheek and left. Tony walked with them downstairs so that he could let them out. Yvette sat up in the bed. She looked over at the clock next to her bed; it was close to 3am. She thought back to that wild chick Tamika; Yvette remembered everything she had said. She looked down at her engagement ring and shook her head. Tonight was supposed to be the happiest night of her life. "Why was she here if she wasn't here with Ray? Tony knew he had planned on proposing to me so if they were messing around why would he invite her? Tony walked in the room just then. Yvette looked up at him as he approached the bed and sat down on the side of her. He leaned in and kissed her. He held her hand and kissed it. "You know I was really scared tonight baby. I was scared we was gon' lose the baby. I really love you Yvette" Tony said. "Tony was any of that true what she was saying? Yvette asked.

Tony looked down he knew that was coming "No baby it wasn't" He replied. "Then why was she so mad at you? Why would she lie? Yvette said. "Yvette I don't know." "I don't believe you Tony. I think you do know. I think she was here for you. I don't believe for a minute especially after the show she put on that she was here with Ray" Yvette said. Tony took a deep breath and exhaled. "Baby let's not do this tonight, you gon, be my wife. You don't have to worry about another woman anymore I promise." He said. "Is she pregnant Tony? I think I have a right to know" Yvette said. "Yvette I told you I don't know" He said "No what you said was no; nothing she said tonight was the truth" Yvette said. "Why was she here? If tonight you knew you were proposing to me why was she here Tony? What kind of games are you playing? Yvette asked.

Tony stood up and ran his fingers through his pretty curly hair. "Baby I'm tired can we please drop this? Tony said. "Hell to the Naw" Yvette said. "Tony I'm pregnant with your child and you proposed to me; I have a right to know dammit!" Yvette demanded. Tony looked at her and said. "Yvette" "I'm not gone back down Tony so you better come with the truth or you can take this engagement ring back" She said. Tony shook his head he was furious and when he saw Tamika again he was gone beat her ass just like he promised. "Baby why you want to do this? Why can't we just be happy for tonight? Tony said. "Well you should have thought about that before you decided to invite yo hoe to our party" Yvette said. Tony was walking around in circles and pacing back and forth "Baby, please let's drop this right now" Tony said. Yvette shook her head and looked down. "Tony if you not gone say anything then I'll take that as an admission of guilt. Let me tell you something right now; I spent six years in a marriage where lies were common and that's not a marriage Tony and I refuse to repeat it. If you can't be honest with me then there's no need for us to get married." Yvette said. "Baby don't say that" Tony said.

Yvette took off Tony's engagement ring and placed it on the side table next to the bed. Tony sighed and said "Ok fine Yvette, if you think this is gon' make you feel better fine I'll tell you. She was here tonight because she likes me and wanna be with me. I've have told her time and time again I have a woman and nobody is coming between us but she won't listen. So I thought if I invited her tonight and she saw me propose to you that she would get the picture and leave me alone." Tony said. "Did you have sex with her? Tony paused before speaking, "No" "Then why would she say she was pregnant by you? Yvette asked. "Yvette I don't know. I just told you how crazy she is. Who knows what's going on inside her head" Yvette looked doubtful at Tony and he said, "baby, I don't know"

"Can we be through with this? I wanna get in the bed with you and hold you." He said. Yvette rolled her eyes. "Can you put the ring back on now boo?" He said. Tony walked over to the table and picked up the ring and placed it back on Yvette's finger. Don't ever take it off again." He said. Tony kissed Yvette and hugged her tight. He wanted her to drop this mess. He didn't want to admit that he'd slept with Tamika many times. In fact the condo she was living in was his. He kept it so he would have a place to see the women he messed around with; that way he had a place to go when he tell Yvette he's out of town. He would really be laying up with Tamika or whoever he wanted in there for the moment. Tony did intend to continue to see Tamika after the wedding but she messed that up. She spoiled her good thing. Tomorrow I'm gon' let her ass know she got until the end of the month to find her a place to stay. He told himself. Tony kissed Yvette on the cheek and said "I'm gone get ready for bed baby I'll be right back" She watched him walk away.

Yvette looked down at her ring she wanted to believe Tony but her experience wouldn't allow it. She wanted so desperately to believe Tamika wasn't pregnant. If she was, then it would ruin her whole experience. It was her first pregnancy and she really wanted to have the baby. The thought of another woman caring her man's baby made her sad. I know he loves me and I truly believe he wants to marry me because he loves the baby and me. I'm so scared this will turn out like my first marriage. Yvette thought to herself. Yvette got up and went to the bathroom to pee while on the toilet she could see Tony in the shower. Life just didn't seem to be working out for her. Again Yvette asked herself "How did I get here? I was supposed to take some time to myself to heal after a long abusive marriage and here I am again back in love with another man who loves to cheat. No he doesn't beat me but the cheating hurts just as much as a fist. God knows I love him and I want to be his wife but I'm so scared of ending up in a dead end marriage again. Lord help me."

December 23rd 2007

Yvette had sent three limos to the airport to pick up her family and Tony's family. She waited at the house for them all to arrive. She had Rosie to set out cheese and meat platters along with little slices of cocktail bread and crackers before dinner. Since today was Rosie's last day she was going to Mexico for a month to visit her family; Yvette had to hire a few extra cooks to cook their holiday meals. Rosie walked in the room to let Yvette know she was leaving. She jumped when she called her name. She was so nervous about meeting Tony's family. Her nerves were shot. Yvette said goodbye to Rosie and gave her a Christmas bonus and she left. She sat down and looked at her watch. She just couldn't relax. She didn't know how Tony's family was going to react to her pregnancy and to their engagement. She had already told her family about the pregnancy and the engagement. She took several deep breaths to try and calm her nerves. She looked around the house. It was still looking beautiful and festive. Yvette decided to make sure everybody's rooms were in order in an effort to calm her nerves. She figured if she started moving she would stop watching the time. Yvette made her rounds and it looked like everything was set. She spent extra time in Tony's family's rooms to make sure they were perfect.

Yvette was starting to feel queasy again she had eaten a light breakfast and Rosie had made her a light lunch. She ate as much as she could eat without getting sick which wasn't much. Since the pregnancy Yvette had lost ten pounds. She nibbled on a saltine cracker as she waited in the family room for their family's to arrive. Tony walked in the room and kissed her on the lips. He tasted the crackers crumbs around her mouth. "Hmm you feeling sick again boo?" He said. "A little" Yvette replied. Tony sat next to Yvette and pulled her in his arms. He rubbed her stomach gently. "How does that feel? He said. Yvette closed her eyes "Hmm that feels good baby" She said. "I can't wait to find out if we having a boy." Tony said. Yvette giggled and said "Or a girl" "Naw" It's a boy" Tony said. "You keep saying that but what if it's a girl? Yvette said. "As long as the baby is healthy I don't care what it is. But it would be nice to have a little boy" He said. They laughed together. Tony and Yvette held hands. Yvette smiled she looked up at Tony and said, "I love you" "I love you too" He responded. They kissed passionately until the phone rang. Tony reached over and answered it "Hello" It was the limo driver letting him know they had picked up both families and was heading to the house. Tony hung up the phone "They are on their way from the airport. You wanna get a quickie in before they get here? He asked. Yvette frowned since she had gotten pregnant sex with Tony was very uncomfortable and painful. She was still feeling a little queasy but she didn't want to let Tony down. "Promise you won't be too rough? She said. Tony kissed Yvette "Baby I promise but you know how I like it. Don't be mad if I can't hold back" He said. Yvette sighed reluctantly she agreed. Tony carried her upstairs.

When Tony got finished Yvette could hardly move. She was crying and holding her stomach. Tony was lying next to her breathing hard. He looked over at her and said, "I'm sorry baby. I'm sorry" Yvette felt her stomach start to turn she got up as fast as she could and walked to the bathroom. She sat on the toilet when she got in the bathroom hoping the queasy feeling would go away but it didn't she stood up and pulled the toilet seat up and threw up. She was gagging so loud Tony ran into the bathroom and kneeled beside her on the toilet.

He held her hair back as she continued to gag and spit. When the queasiness passed Tony wet a towel and held it to her face and held her in his arms. Yvette lay against Tony as he rocked her with her eyes closed. Before long the queasy feeling was back and she was throwing up again. Yvette was gagging so hard she felt like she was throwing up all of her insides. When she was finished she was so weak Tony had to help her walk out of the bathroom. He washed her up and helped her change her clothes and put her to bed. Yvette lay there praying she wouldn't get sick again. As soon as she thought that she began to gag and heave. Tony came running out of the bathroom and held her up but nothing was coming up. When it passed Tony went in the bathroom and grabbed the garbage can and put it beside the bed for Yvette to throw up in. He heard the doorbell and knew their families had arrived. He looked at Yvette as she lay over the side of the bed. "I'll be right back baby" Tony ran downstairs to open the door.

The first one to greet him was his mother "Hello son. What took you so long to open the door huh?" She spoke with an island accent. She hugged and kissed him. Eva Riche was a beautiful woman. She looked like she was mixed. She was light skinned with long beautiful black hair. She was not very small but not fat either she was in between. Tony's brother Mark was with her along with his wife Kim and their two girls. His sister was unable to make it. Yvette's mother and sisters and their husbands and kids were all there. "Where's Yvette? Her mother asked Tony. "She's laying down upstairs but she'll be down in a minute" He said. He didn't want Yvette's nosey mother all in their bedroom messing with her. He directed the drivers to put all the luggage by the door because he didn't know which rooms

Yvette had assigned to whom so he would let her deal with it when she felt better. Tony had everybody to go in the family room where Yvette had refreshments set up, the meat and cheese and cracker tray along with bottled water, juice and cocktails for anyone who wanted it. She also had cookies and brownies and milk for the kids and chips and dip. Yvette was just getting up she still felt queasy but she knew she had to make an appearance or her mother and sisters would be up in her bedroom in a minute. She went into the bathroom and washed her face and brushed her teeth. Tony had changed her clothes she was wearing a pink and silver velour Juicy Couture outfit. She put on her matching pink and silver Juicy shoes and touched up her makeup. Yvette looked in the mirror she still looked pale but she looked presentable. She walked slowly downstairs to greet her family and her mother in-law to be.

Yvette entered the family room and her mother was the first one to see her. "Hey there's my baby" She jumped up and hugged Yvette; Yvette's sisters crowded around her. "Aw look at her she got that pregnant look" Lawnyae stated. "Come on and sit down sweetie." Her mother said. "I will in a minute mama. I haven't met Tony's mother yet." Yvette said. Eva was sitting on the love seat watching Yvette with surprise written all over her face. She's pregnant? What is Tony thinking? Hmm ... she's very pretty. Tony always did love beautiful women. And he always was a sucker for em to. She's

64

probably faking this pregnancy. And if she is pregnant it's probably not his. These American women would say and do anything to get a man with money. Eva thought to herself. Tony was watching his mother's reaction to Yvette. It was just as he thought; she didn't approve which is why he didn't tell her about their engagement or the baby. Tony spoke up "Mama this Yvette, my fiancée" The look that crossed Eva's face was undeniable not only was she shocked but she didn't approve. Yvette couldn't help but miss that disapproving look she had just received. This is what she had been dreading. Oh my God she hates me. That's why I told Tony he should have told his mother weeks ago about our engagement and the baby. Yvette thought to herself. Yvette stretched her hand out "It's nice to meet you Mrs. Riche" Eva looked down at Yvette's hand and back up at her before she shook it. And even then she acted like she really didn't want to touch her.

Tony turned to his younger brother "And this is my brother Mark and his wife Kim and their kids Mia and Sasha. The little one is name Sasha she's five the bigger one is Mia she's seven. Yvette smiled at the children they were beautiful little girls. Tony's brother Mark was handsome but not as handsome as Tony was. His wife was dark skinned with shoulder length hair. She was average looking but she was nice and so was his brother. Yvette tried to ignore Eva's reaction to her and pay attention to her guests. Yvette went and sat beside her mother and sister. "Oh look at you; you look pale. Are you feeling sick?" Yvette's mother asked. "Yeah I've been feeling queasy" Yvette said. "You need to eat some saltines or some dry toast." Octavia stated. "I've been eating saltines all day but the queasy feeling keeps coming back." Yvette said. "Well that's going to happen honey it's called morning sickness." Her mother said. "Are you all hungry? Help yourself to the meat and cheese tray." Yvette said out loud to everyone.

Demetrius and Mario got up and walked over to the tray and started eating. Tony and Mark walked over and joined them. He introduced his brother to Mario and Demetrius and he started pouring drinks. Yvette attempted to make Eva and Kim feel comfortable. "We have a little time before dinner did you guys wanna go upstairs and get settled in your rooms? She asked. "Yes, that's a good idea" Kim responded. Eva didn't respond. Yvette's mother looked over at her and whispered to her daughters "She's rude" Yvette nudged her mother's arm to silence her; she didn't want Eva to hear what she said. Yvette got up and said, "Honey, can you and the guys bring everybody's bags upstairs? Tony frowned and said "Baby what about all those extra housekeepers you hired," Yvette smiled and said. "Um sweetie they're not housekeepers they're cooks and it was only two of them." "Humph!" Eva said. Yvette looked over at her. Oh no she didn't. Yvette thought to herself. Yvette tried to ignore Eva. She continued to talk to Tony. "Honey can you please get the bags? Tony set his drink down and the other guys followed him out of the room. "If you all would follow me I'll show you where you'll be sleeping." Yvette said. Everybody followed Yvette out of the room. She walked past Tony and the guys as they were trying to sort out the bags. They walked up the stairs and Yvette showed each person where they would be sleeping. Eva seemed ok with the room Yvette had chosen for her. It was big and roomy and one of the best rooms in the house. All of the rooms were nice but some were a little more lavish than the others. She made certain to assign those rooms to her mother and Eva.

Tony and the guys got all of the bags in their respective rooms and they rushed back downstairs to finish their cocktails. Yvette left her family alone to settle in their rooms and get comfortable before dinner. She went in her room and lay down; she was tired and feeling a little weak. She picked up the phone by the bed and called Krystal. Krystal was in LA visiting her brother and mother. Tonya had flown home to Detroit for Christmas to be with her family also. "Hello" "Hey Krissy" Yvette said sounding weak. "Hey boo, how are you?" Krystal said. "Girl tired and weak" Yvette said. "Have you eaten anything today?" Krystal asked. "Yeah I had a light breakfast," Yvette said. "What does a light breakfast consist of Yvette? Krystal said. "Girl I had some dry toast and grapefruit and a scrambled eggs" Yvette said. "Did you eat it all? She asked. "No, I ate the toast and some of the grapefruit and a little bit of the eggs" Yvette responded. "What did you eat for lunch? Krystal asked. "I had a bowl of soup and crackers. It was chicken noodle." Yvette said. Krystal laughed, "Am I sounding like your mother? She said. "Yeah, shit" Yvette said. "I'm sorry but I just want my girl to take care of herself" Krystal said.

"I know" Yvette said. "What's wrong girl" Yvette took a deep breath and exhaled "It's Tony's mother" Yvette said. "What about her?" Krystal asked. "She doesn't like me" Yvette said. "How do you know she don't like you? "Girl she made it real obvious. She acted like she didn't want to shake my hand when Tony introduced us and you should have seen the look on her face when he announced to her that we're engaged. It's very obvious she didn't approve" Yvette said. "Wait a minute you mean she didn't know before today that you two were engaged? Krystal said. "Nope, I've been telling Tony for weeks to call his mother and tell her so she wouldn't be shocked when she got here. But nope, he kept saying he was gon' get around to it" "Hmm he foul for that one" Krystal said. "I know right" "Well Yvette just try and give her the benefit of the doubt. She's going to be your mother in-law. And try not to worry too much girl" "I know your right. Yvette said.

Yvette felt another wave of queasiness and she held her stomach and said. "I hope this queasiness goes away before dinner. I would like to enjoy a meal" "Lay down and get some rest and maybe it will" Krystal said. "Ok, enough about me and my problems what's going on with you? Are you enjoying your family?" Yvette asked. "As a matter of fact I am. "Ok what's going on I can hear that smile in your voice" Yvette said. Krystal laughed, "Girl is it that obvious. My brother invited one of his friends over for dinner and oh he is fine and he's digging me girl. Pray for me Yvette girl it's been a long time since I had my world rocked and the way this brother keeps looking at me girl I don't know. This might be the night I break my vow of chastity!" Krystal said.

Yvette and Krystal both laughed "Girl you so crazy. You ain't giving up nutin' tonight or any night you're going to stick to your vow to wait on God" Yvette said. "That's what I'm saying Yvette girl I might break that vow tonight I'm telling you. Whew pray for a sista. But girl I got to go he's looking this way with those pretty eyes. I'll call you later tonight ok. Take care sweetie, love you" Krystal said. "Love you to girl bye" Yvette hung up the phone. She dialed Tonya's number to see what she was up to. Tonya didn't answer her phone so Yvette left her a message "What's up Lady T? I was just calling to see how you're enjoying your family, didn't want nothing really. Holla at you later bye." Yvette put the phone down and grabbed the remote and turned on the TV. She heard a knock at the door. "Come in" It was her family coming to check on her. They entered the room and were amazed at how big and beautiful it was. "Wow Tony really has a beautiful house," Robin stated. They all sat on the bed with her. They talked and laughed for hours just catching up with each other. Soon the cook announced over the intercom that dinner was ready and they all headed downstairs to eat.

By the time Yvette got Tony and the guys out of the family room they were all tipsy, talking loud and laughing. Tony sat at one end of the table and Yvette sat at the other. Yvette was going to ask Tony to bless the food but since he was damn near drunk she decided to bless the food herself. "Can we all stand and hold hands please" Everybody stood and did as she asked "Oh heavenly father bless this meal we are about to receive. Bless the cooks who worked so hard to prepare it. We ask that you please remove any infirmities from the food. We ask that you allow it to nourish our bodies. Lord we thank you for allowing us all to come together during this Holiday season. We thank you for blessing everyone to make it here safely and we thank you in advance for blessing them all to make it back home safe and sound. Lord we give you all the honor the praise and the glory in Jesus name Amen."

"That was a beautiful prayer Yvette." Kim said. "Thank you." They all sat down and began to serve their selves. They were eating prime rib, roasted garlic mashed potatoes, French cut green beans and garlic bread. They also had a cream of chicken and broccoli soup and a salad. It was a very lavish meal as good as any meal you would get in a five star restaurant. As everyone ate and talked Yvette looked around; it was nice to have her mother and sisters there with her especially with the way Tony's mother was acting. Yvette looked down the table at her; she was sitting next to Tony. She was talking to Tony about something. The more Yvette watched she noticed she wasn't talking to him she seemed to be scolding him about something and that worried her. She wondered what it could be. Tony looked up and noticed Yvette watching them. He smiled at her "Everything taste good baby" Eva looked over at Yvette; she straightened up in her chair and started to eat her food. Whatever they were talking about Tony didn't want Yvette to know. She tried to put a smile on her face so she wouldn't alarm her mother and sisters. After dinner Tony took the guys to his recreation room and he showed the kids to the game room. Yvette invited the women in the theater room to watch a movie. Yvette didn't really feel like watching a movie but she wanted to be a good hostess. All she felt like doing was going to bed. Eva declined the movie she went right up to her room for the rest of the evening. Kim however stayed with the rest of the women and they all had a delightful time together.

The ladies watched two movies and Yvette was out like a light before the end of the first movie. By 11:30 p.m. the women were ready to retire to bed. Tony and the guys came in the room as the women were leaving. Yvette was still passed out on the couch. Her mother was trying to wake her up when Tony walked in. Tony and the guys were drunk by now and were ready to watch his video of his last fight. Tony saw Yvette and said "Oh don't worry about it Ms. Mitchell, I'll get her" Tony walked over and picked Yvette up and carried her in his arms to their bedroom. Even though he was drunk he was extra careful with her. When he got her in the room he undressed her and put on her pajamas. He pulled the covers back and Yvette got in the bed. "Where's everybody?" Yvette said still half asleep. "They went to bed baby. Lie down and go back to sleep" He said.

Yvette obeyed and before Tony left the room she was sound asleep. He turned the TV on he knew Yvette didn't like sleeping in the dark unless he was in the room with her. He left the room and closed the door behind him. Her mother and sister were waiting in the hall by the door when he came out. "Is she sleeping? They asked. Tony responded "Yeah" "Well we won't bother her we just wanted to say goodnight. We'll see her in the morning." Tony nodded and they all walked away. The ladies went to their rooms and Tony went back downstairs to join the men. They stayed up for hours talking and laughing and watching his fights and then movies. When Tony came to bed it was 3 a.m. in the morning. Yvette was still asleep after he took his shower and joined her in the bed. Tony pulled Yvette into his arms and they both slept like babies.

Los Angeles Christmas Eve 2007

Krystal was sitting at the breakfast table with her mother and her niece and nephew. Curtis had not come down to join them yet. They were talking about what stores they were going to hit up to do their last minute shopping. The kids usually spent Christmas Eve at home with Marissa but this year she ran off to Hawaii with her boyfriend and wouldn't be back until after New Year's. Curtis was waiting in the family room for Pam to arrive. She was joining them on their shopping spree. Curtis's cell phone rang it was Pam letting him know she was in the driveway. Curtis went and opened the front door. The weather outside was beautiful it was 62 degrees out. Pam walked up to the door and hugged Curtis they kissed each other. Curtis brought her inside and went straight to the kitchen. As they walked in Pam said "Good morning everybody" They all greeted her, then Curtis made the introductions. He invited Pam to sit down and have breakfast with them. They all felt at ease with Pam. She was an easy person to talk to. She was very simple not extravagant like most of the women Curtis had dated. She was humble and down to earth. After breakfast they all got their jackets and headed out. Curtis and Pam rode in his car and Krystal drove everybody else in Curtis's truck.

When they got to the mall they split up. Curtis and Pam went their own way and Ashley, Lil' Curtis, Krystal and Delores stayed together. Krystal passed by a baby store and just had to go in. She had given Yvette and Tonya their gifts but she couldn't resist looking at the baby clothes and thinking of Yvette's baby. She couldn't wait until she had the baby. Krystal had never been able to be at the hospital when her niece and nephew were born but she planned to be there every step of the way with Yvette. Krystal couldn't help but feel a longing, a longing for her own family. She wanted a husband and kids of her own. She had really grown tired of waiting for Mr. Right. She almost allowed herself to sleep with her brother's friend but she was able to get a grip on her hormones. Since then it seem like something had stirred up inside of her. She knew she wanted to be happy and the only way she knew for sure she would be happy was to wait for God to send her the man he had for her. Krystal had been through a lot of men in college and she had gotten hurt every time.

She'd dated men she met through her job at the radio station but those relationships didn't work out either. So now here she was single and unattached. In a way she envied Yvette not because she wanted Tony but because she had somebody willing to share his life with her even though he was a lying cheating dog; at least she got somebody to propose to her twice.

Delores wondered what they were doing in the baby store. "Um young lady why are we in this baby store? Is there something you want to tell me?" Delores asked. Krystal looked over at her mother and smiled and shook her head. "No ma I just wanted to look. I was looking to see if I saw something cute for Yvette" Krystal said. "She's pregnant?" Delores asked. Krystal sighed and said, "Yes she is." "Oh how nice for her" Delores said. "What is she having a boy or a girl? Her mother asked. "Actually she doesn't know yet. She hasn't had her ultrasound" "What is she hoping for? Delores asked. "Actually I don't think she cares as long as the baby is healthy." Krystal said. "Well that's a good way of looking at it" Delores said. "Yeah" Krystal continued to look around the store. She realized it would be impossible to buy anything for the baby because she didn't know if it was a boy or a girl. Krystal just had to buy something so she chose some nice receiving blankets and Onesies.

Curtis and Pam walked hand in hand as they strolled the streets on Rodeo Drive. "Your family is very nice" Pam commented. "Yes, they are" Curtis was quiet as they walked and looked in different shops and it was making Pam uncomfortable. Curtis had never been so quiet before he always had something to say or he was always cracking a joke or something. "Are you ok?" Curtis frowned and looked at Pam "Yeah why do you ask? "You seem distant like you have something on your mind" Curtis shook his head no "I'm ok" He said. Pam sighed and dropped the subject. His cell phone rang "Hello" It was Marissa and she was crying. "Curtis I need you to send me some money" Curtis stopped walking. "Send you some money for what? He asked. "I had a fight with my friend and I was on my way home when some guy snatched my purse. I have nothing no credit cards, no money not even my pass port" "How much do you need? He said. "I need about three grand to pay for my ticket" "Alright I'll wire you the money." He said. Marissa gave him the

71

information for the wire. Curtis wrote all the information down and ended the call. He looked at Pam. She was looking at him wondering who he was talking to. "That was Marissa, my ex-wife; she's stranded in Hawaii and needs me to wire her some money to get home. I'm going to have to go to the bank to make this wire transfer." He said. Curtis called Krystal and told her what was going on. He intended to wire the money and come back and meet them. Curtis and Pam walked back to his car.

As Curtis drove to the bank Pam sat quietly staring out the window. She wanted to ask Curtis some questions but she didn't want to offend him but she had to know. "Why is she stranded?" Curtis looked at Pam. "She said somebody snatched her purse" He responded. "Wasn't she traveling with a friend?" Pam asked. "Um yeah but she said they had a fight" Curtis said. Pam looked out the window then back at Curtis. "Her friend couldn't help her out? Pam asked. "I don't know," He said. "Well why didn't you ask?" Pam said. "Look do you have a problem with me helping her?" Curtis said. She stared at him before she answered. "No I just wondered why you're so eager to jump to her aid without asking any questions" Pam said. "Because she's the mother of my children and because she's stranded" Curtis said. "So that makes it ok? She asked. "Pam what's the problem?" Curtis asked. "Well I guess I'm just wondering if you always just drop everything and run to help her. I mean she is your Ex-wife. And what kind of friend is she traveling with who would just leave her high and dry like that?" Pam asked. Curtis sighed, "I don't know Pam. I don't know the kind of company she keeps." He said. "Was she with a man?" Pam asked. Curtis glanced at Pam and said. "Yeah she was" "Look Curtis if you feel like you still have feelings for your ex-wife I wish you would let me know.

I don't want to get into this relationship with you and have to constantly be competing with her" Pam was starting to annoy him. "Pam I'm not in love with Marissa but she is the mother of my kids and there are certain things that I'll do for her. If you have a problem with that then I don't know what to tell you" Curtis said. "Are you still sleeping with her?" Curtis paused before answering. "Why are you asking me that?" He said. "Because I want to know; are you still sleeping with her?" She asked. "No" He said. "Hmm I don't believe you" Pam said. "Well you can believe what you want to believe Pam I told you the truth," He said. Curtis pulled into the bank parking lot and got out of the car without saying a word to Pam. She didn't move to follow him she just waited in the car. When Curtis returned to the car he apologized to Pam. "I'm sorry for the way I spoke to you but I just don't understand why you have a problem with Marissa. She's not a problem for me but as the mother of my kids I owe her a certain amount of respect" He said. "And you know what Curtis I agree. Respect her I would think less of you if you didn't but what you don't have to do is be at her every beck and call, now that I have a problem with. This is the second time I've been with you and she's called and needed your immediate help and now you're telling me she's not a problem for you" Pam said.

"I'm telling you she's not a problem because it's the truth." Curtis said. "Alright fine Curtis" Pam said. Curtis started the car up and pulled away from the bank. As he was driving he looked over at Pam and said "Do you want me to just take you back to my house so you can get your car?" Pam looked at Curtis suspiciously "Is that what you want to do? She said. "You seem upset so if you want to leave I'll understand" Curtis said. Pam laughed "Oh I see I've made you mad and now you don't want to be bothered? Well I don't think you wanted to be bothered with me in the first place. You've been distant all morning anyway so yeah why don't you take me to get my car" Pam said. "Fine with me" Curtis said. They rode all the way to Curtis house without saying another word to each other.

When Curtis pulled in his driveway Pam got out of the car without saying a word to him. He waited until she was in her car and pulling out of the driveway before he pulled off. He decided to go by his office for a while. Curtis sat in his empty office on Christmas Eve afternoon. He didn't really have any work to do he just wanted to be alone. For some reason he wasn't feeling the Holiday spirit. His cell phone rang. Curtis picked it up and answered it. "Hello" It was Marissa. "Hello Curtis, did you wire the money? "Yeah I did" He gave her the wire information to retrieve the money. "Curtis can you be a sweetie and pick me up from the airport?" "Yeah, what time? "9 pm from LAX" "I'll be there" Marissa poured on the sweetness "Alright sweetie I can't wait to see you" "Alright talk to you later."

Krystal and Delores and the kids waited for Curtis and Pam at their favorite restaurant. The kids were hungry so Krystal told them to go ahead and order. Krystal called Curtis's cell phone. "Hello" "Hey man where the heck are you?" Krystal asked. "Oh I'm sorry um Pam wanted to go home so I had to drive her back to my house so she could get her car. Then I decided to come back to the office to get some work done" Curtis said. "But I thought you said you had to wire Marissa some money? "Oh yeah I did that and after that she wanted to go home" Krystal knew he wasn't telling the whole story. "Well we're sitting in the restaurant waiting on you" Krystal said. "Y'all go ahead and finish up and I'll see y'all at the house" He said. After talking to Krystal his mind wandered to his childhood and all the abuse from his father.

He always thought about his father around this time of the year. He thought about their last meeting and the things his father had said to him. The words really hurt. He thought back to that day hearing those words over and over in his mind "I hate you; I curse the day you were born. I should have drowned you in the bathtub." It confused him how he could allow those words to have any effect on him after how his father treated him he felt like he shouldn't care what he thought of him. "Why me? Why didn't he love me? What's wrong with me?" Curtis sat at his desk for hours just thinking. When finally he decided to leave it was 6:00 p.m. He called home and Krystal answered the phone "Hello" She said. "Hey Krystal what's up? He said. "Christmas Eve where are you?" She asked sounding annoyed. "I'm sorry the time got away from me. I have to pick Marissa up from the airport at 9pm so I'm just gone stay out until then" "Hurry up you're missing the family fun," she said. "I know but I'll be home soon." Curtis left his office and went to the bar. He drank until it was time to pick up Marissa.

Curtis sat in his car at the LAX airport waiting on Marissa. Marissa exited the terminal and saw Curtis's car. She walked right up to the car and opened the door. "Hey sweetie" She said. Curtis looked up in surprise his mind was a million miles away and he didn't see her walk up to the car. "Hey Marissa" Curtis got out of the car and helped her with her luggage. Then he opened the passenger side door for her. Before she got in she held his chin in her hand and kissed his lips. Curtis closed the door and walked around to the driver side. He looked at Marissa and she looked at him seductively. "Do you want to come over to the house?" He asked. "Sure why not? She said. Twenty minutes later Curtis and Marissa walked through the front door of his house. "Everybody is probably in the family room." He said to Marissa. Marissa stopped walking and said, "Who is everybody? "Um your kids and my sister and mother" He responded. Marissa frowned up "Oh I didn't know they were here" "Yes it is Christmas. Are you coming?" He said. Marissa thought about it. "You know what Curtis I'm very tired so why don't I just crash here tonight? Is it ok if I just go upstairs and lay down?" She asked. Curtis stared at her for a moment. He knew what she wanted and he wanted to give it to her. "Go ahead" He said. Marissa winked at him and walked up stairs. Curtis watched her as she walked away then he walked away and into the family room. Curtis joined his family for the rest of the evening. He didn't mention that Marissa was upstairs and at 12:30am everybody went to bed. When Curtis walked into his bedroom he saw Marissa passed out on his bed butt-naked. He wasn't surprised he knew she would be waiting for him. He took a shower and crawled in bed next to her as naked as she was.

Atlanta Christmas Morning 2007

It was 10:30 a.m. Christmas morning. The tradition in Yvette's family is to shower and get dressed and have breakfast then everybody open their gifts. Yvette had made sure Tony conveyed that message to his family. He said that wouldn't be a problem because they did Christmas morning the same way. Yvette was the last one to come downstairs. She was trying to hurry but her morning sickness wouldn't allow it. But everybody understood giving her condition, everybody except Tony's mother. She hadn't warmed up to Yvette at all since she'd been there. She barely said two words to Yvette. Yvette had attempted to talk to her several times but she gave her short answers to her questions and just her body language and facial expressions said she didn't want to be bothered so she left her alone. As she walked into the family room Eva made that rude sound she usually makes when anyone compliments Yvette "Hmph" Yvette was feeling too sick and tired to put up with Eva this morning. She looked over at Eva and rolled her eyes and didn't care what anybody in the room thought. Tony had noticed the tension between his mother and Yvette but he never said anything. He pretty much ignored it hoping it would go away. Although he didn't like the way his mother was treating his future wife he didn't have the balls to stand up to her. Tony held out his arm for Yvette to come and sit by him. She walked over and sat down next to him. He put his arm around her and kissed her on the cheek. "Good morning baby. Merry Christmas" Yvette smiled weakly. "Good morning honey"

Yvette rested her head on Tony's shoulders as the gifts were passed out and everyone began to open their gifts. Tony placed his gift in Yvette's lap. Yvette opened the box it was a picture she turned it over and saw it was a picture of an office. It was a beautiful. Yvette looked at Tony confused. "What is this honey?" "It is a picture of your new office" "My new office. Where is it located?" "Right down the hall from our bedroom. So you can have your own space to work. And if you don't feel like going to work you can work from home" "How?" Yvette asked. "It's set up so you can broadcast from home" "But how?" Yvette asked. "I spoke to Krystal and she set something up to where you can work from home when things get to be too much for you in your later months of pregnancy" Tony said. "Wow honey that is really thoughtful of you. This will come in handy now cuz it's a lot of days I don't feel like going to work" Yvette said. "It's ready when you are baby" Yvette hugged and kissed Tony. "I love you baby," Yvette said. "I love you to boo" "Now for your gift."

"Can you hand me that small box over there honey?" Yvette pointed to the tree. Tony got up and grabbed the box and handed it to Yvette. She handed it to him and said, "Here it's for you open it" Tony opened the box and removed the tissue paper. He picked up the photo. "Baby what's this?" He asked. Yvette smiled at him. "It's a picture of your baby" Tony looked at Yvette and smiled "It is. He said. Where's the baby I can't see it." He said. Yvette pointed at the picture. "This is the head and this is the arm and here you can see the leg and the feet and here is his penis." She said. Tony looked at Yvette with a huge smile on his face. "Baby it's a boy" He asked. Yvette smiled and nodded. Tony jumped up and announced to the room "It's a boy. I'm having a boy." Up until now everyone was into their gifts and wasn't paying Yvette and Tony any attention. They all clapped and cheered for Tony and Yvette. All except for Eva she had been watching Tony and Yvette the whole time. She didn't like the way he doted on her. Eva had never seen Tony so taken with a woman before. It was clear her son loved this one and that pissed her off. She didn't feel Yvette was good enough for her son. She had her heart set on Tony marrying his childhood sweetheart a girl from the islands where he was from not this American trash. "Mama it's a boy!" Eva tried to paste a smile on her face for her son's sake; she failed miserably. The rest of the family was genuinely happy for them. They all spent the rest of the day just sitting around talking and laughing and waiting on dinner.

Los Angeles Christmas Morning 2007

Krystal, Curtis and their mother along with Ashley and Lil Curtis and Marissa all sat around the Christmas tree that morning opening gifts. Marissa didn't come with any gifts for anyone but her kids had gifts for her and so did Delores. Everyone had something to open. After that they all got dressed and met back downstairs for breakfast. Later that afternoon Delores's sister Lee and her husband and Lee's daughter and son and their families joined them. It had been years since Krystal and Curtis had seen their cousins. They had a good time catching up with each other. Aunt Helen came with more gifts for everyone. The kids put on a talent show for the adults and they were actually pretty good. Everyone enjoyed their skits. Soon it was time for dinner. They all ate at Curtis's long dining table so there was no need for a kid's table. It was better this way because everybody was able to communicate with one another and they all had a wonderful time. The food was excellent and desert was even better. Stuffed to the gills they all sat around in the movie room watching the new releases Curtis had gotten his hands on. All in all Christmas was fabulous for the Abney family.

Detroit Michigan Christmas Day 2007

Christmas morning went a little different at the Lewis' house. All of the kids woke up the adults at 8 a.m. and they all staggered out of bed to watch the kids open their gifts. Then the kids played while the ladies showered and started cooking Christmas dinner. Breakfast was a bowl of cold cereal or fruit from the fruit basket. By mid-morning the ladies would set out a veggie tray and a meat and cheese tray for those who missed out on that bowl of cereal and just for snacking to tide them all over until dinner. By 2 p.m. the Christmas cookies were set out for all to enjoy. And by 4 p.m. dinner was ready. The adults sat at one table and the kids had their own table. By 6 p.m. family and friends were arriving and they would play spades and bid whiz and by 7 p.m. the adults old enough to drink would be drinking and by 8 p.m. the adults who had a bit too much to drink were usually arguing and fighting and by 10 p.m. they would make up and everything was everything. And this was Christmas in the Lewis household.

Chicago Christmas Day 2007

Leonard joined his parents at their house along with his brother and his new wife and their newborn baby. Leonard sat back and watched his parent's "Ohh and aw" over the new baby, his niece. It made him sick to his stomach to watch them praise Leroy and not him. As usual he had out done Leonard and it pissed him off. If that bitch Yvette had stayed home I would be the one celebrating my new baby but no she had to run her ass away to Atlanta. Now she's lying up with that big stupid goon Tony and having his damn baby. He thought to himself. It wasn't fair and he wanted to hit something or somebody. Leonard looked at his brother and thought better of it. His father would only get upset and put him out. This was a terrible Christmas for Leonard and all he wanted to do was hop on the next thing smoking and head to Atlanta and knock on Tony's door and shoot him in the face then beat Yvette until she loss that damn baby and drag her ass home. That idea was starting to lift Leonard's spirits. I might have to make that happen. He thought to himself. Leonard sat in the corner with an odd little smile on his face. If he parents had noticed that wicked smile they would have been worried.

Atlanta December 27th 2006

Yvette was in her office working on the event Diva Promotions was having on the 31st. Krystal was handling the celebrities and their managers and Tonya was handling the promotions side of it. She was making sure every radio station including theirs was plugging their party. She made sure all signs were posted on every corner in every bar and at every club and transit stations. Yvette was handling the location business making sure there were no problems with the venue and making sure deposits were made and going over the seating charts and stage set ups. She was also in charge of choosing their wardrobe for the evening in addition to Tony's. Yvette was so tired but she kept working. Her mother had brought up a sandwich for her a little while ago that she had not eaten yet. All Yvette wanted to do was go to sleep but she had to finish going over the details at least before she lay down. Kim passed by Yvette's office door and she stopped. She looked at Yvette before she decided to knock on the door to alert her of her presence. Yvette looked up when she heard Kim knocking on the door. "Oh hi Kim, come in" Yvette said. Kim walked in the office and closed the door behind her. "What's up?" Yvette said. "Nothing I was just passing by and saw you in here and I just thought I would stop and say hi. How are you feeling?" Kim asked.

Yvette put down her pen and ran her fingers through her hair. "Truthfully I'm tired and feeling weak and nauseated" Kim laughed "Yeah that's morning sickness." Yvette laughed and nodded her head. "Yvette I wanted to tell you not to be intimidated by Eva. I see she's giving you a hard time but don't let her get to you. The most important thing for you to do right now is to take care of yourself. I can see you have enough stress on you without the added stress of Eva. Believe me I know how she is. She was the same way with me when Mark and I first got married. Girl she worried me so that I miscarried our first baby. Tony and Mark really place a lot of emphasis on what their mother thinks and want. I know it's hard but try to relax around her she can smell fear. Let her know you're not afraid of her and you're not gonna be pushed around by her. She won't leave you alone but she'll back off and she'll respect you" Kim said. "Wow thank you so much Kim for that information. It's bothered me that Eva doesn't like me and it bothers me even more that Tony won't say anything or do anything about it" Yvette said. "I know honey but that's how they are where their mother is concerned. She has some kind of hold on them and she works it to her advantage. I think what's bothering her is how taken Tony is with you. He's usually not like this with his women and that's how his mother likes it. She encourages them to have more than one woman that's why it comes so easy to him. I spent many years working on Mark and deprogramming him from all the bullshit his mother put in his head. She really doesn't like us American women. She wants her sons to be with island women, women that grew up in their village. So just hang in there Yvette and don't let her get the best of you" Kim said. Yvette stood up and walked toward Kim and hugged her. "Thank you so much Kim. This means a lot to me. It feels so good to have someone from that camp on my side" Yvette said. "Aw Tony is on your side he just don't know how to handle his mother that's all. One thing is for sure he loves you and she can't stand it" Kim said. Yvette hugged her again. "Kim you don't know what this has done for me. I really thank you. You've lifted a load off of my mind" Yvette said. "Us American girls have to stick together. Well I'll let you get back to work but remember what I said Yvette; you take care of yourself and don't let Eva win." Yvette nodded and Kim walked to the door and opened it and left.

Yvette sat down in her chair feeling a little better. She picked up the sandwich her mother had made and took a bite of it; it was turkey and cheddar cheese and mayo her favorite. She had eaten a half of the sandwich when she felt it getting ready to come back up. She ran to the bathroom in her office and threw up. Yvette knelt in front of the toilet holding the base of it waiting for the nausea to go away. When she was sure it was gone she got up and rinsed her mouth out and brushed her teeth. When she came out of the bathroom Eva was sitting on the couch in her office waiting for her. Yvette stopped when she saw Eva. Eva was regarding her with interest. "Come on and sit down child. Don't just stand there. A woman in your condition needs all the rest she can get." Eva said in her island accent. It struck Yvette as strange that Eva was being nice to her and more importantly that she was speaking to her. Yvette walked over to her desk trying to remember the conversation she'd just had with

Kim.

"Hi Eva, what can I do for you? Yvette asked. "Well child I came to see what I could do for you. I know I have behaved rudely since I've been here and I wanted to apologize for that. And as a peace offering I bought you a cup of jasmine tea. It's what us women in the islands drink when we are pregnant and feeling sickness. It'll ease the tummy. I had to search high and low here to find it but finally I found a store that sold it. I hope it'll work for you my dear and I hope we can become friends. I want to be a part of my grandson's life." Eva stood up and walked toward Yvette with the cup of tea in her hand. She sat it on a coaster on Yvette's desk. "Here you go Dear heart. Go ahead and drink up."

Yvette was a little skeptical about it at first. She smelled it; it smelled like jasmine. Then she tasted it and it tasted fine so she drank it in small swallows. Eva made small talk as Yvette sipped her tea in between their conversation. Yvette drank most of the tea then sat the cup down on her desk. Eva looked over in her cup and said "Oh no dear heart you must finish it all for it to have any effect on your sickness" She said. Yvette was already feeling queasy so she assumed Eva was right so she drank the rest of the tea. Eva stood there and watched her with a smile on her face. "There now child don't you feel better already? Yvette lied and said "You know what, I do" "Good child now I'll leave you alone to get your work done and I'll just take this cup back downstairs to the kitchen for cleaning." Eva turned and walked away but then she turned back around and said, "I'm glad we had this time together huh." Yvette nodded "Me too" she was swallowing hard to try and stop the tea from coming back up. Eva smiled and walked out of the office. Yvette waited until she was down the stairs and out of earshot before she closed the door and locked it and ran into the bathroom and threw up the tea. Her stomach was rolling with cramps afterward. She walked out of the bathroom and back to her desk. Yvette sat down hoping the cramps would stop. A few minutes later she ran back into the bathroom throwing up again. She had thrown up so much from that tea her stomach muscles were so sore. Yvette put her work away and went to her bedroom and lay down. She dosed off to sleep.

As Eva put the coffee mug in the kitchen sink she smiled as she thought to herself. That American bitch will not bare any grandson of mine. She'll lose that baby and Tony will lose her and marry Eleshia like he was supposed to. It's only a matter of time now. I can't wait to hear her screaming in pain from labor pains and soon after that the baby will pass through her womb and it'll be all over. Eva told herself. She walked out of the kitchen and went to find Tony. She didn't want to be anywhere near Yvette when she miscarried the baby. Everyone in the house knew she hated Yvette so she wanted to make sure Tony wouldn't blame her so she stuck close to him so he would think she had anything to do with it. She joined the guys in Tony's recreation room they were shooting pool and drinking beer and watching the sports channel. When she entered the room the guys greeted her but they all seemed a bit uncomfortable with her presence. Eva walked pass the pool table and over to the bar and sat down. Tony and Mark looked at each other and the other guys tried not to pay attention. Mark walked over to his mother and asked "Mom what's up?" Eva patted her son on the cheek and said "No worries son" Mark looked back at Tony who was watching but trying to pretend he wasn't.

"Where are the other ladies?" "Oh I don't know boy. Why do you question your mama?" "No reason mama I just wondered why you're hanging out down here with the men?" "Can't a mother come and sit with her boys without you wondering what's wrong? You know I haven't sat with the women since I've been here. So why do you question me now son?" Eva said in the Island accent of hers. "Well mama you know me and Tony don't mind but we don't want the other guys to feel uncomfortable around you. You know they may not be able to say what they want because there's a lady present." Mark said. "Well goot, they shouldn't be speaking in such a way. Now go, run along back to your pool game." Eva pushed Mark away. Mark walked back over to the pool table and shrugged as Tony looked at him. Tony wasn't about to go over there and start bugging her after the way she pushed Mark away she meant business she wasn't about to leave no matter who was uncomfortable. The guys went ahead with their pool game with less enthusiasm than before.

Ernestine and her daughters walked through the front door. Kim was sitting in the front living room reading a book. The kids raced pass with shopping bags in their hands. They ran straight to the game room with the new games Ernestine had purchased for them. The ladies greeted Kim "Hey Kim, how are you?" Kim smiled and responded, "Fine how are you? How was the shopping?" Ernestine replied "Oh it was nice but hectic; everybody's rushing around trying to return gifts and all. Whew I'm tired I think I'll go and lie down for a while" Ernestine looked at Kim and asked, "Where's Yvette? Kim replied "Oh she's up in her office working" Robin looked at her watch "Still it's almost 3:30 p.m. when we left here it was what 11:00 a.m." Lawnyae responded "Let's go in and check on her on our way to the room" The others agreed and they all walked upstairs carrying their shopping bags. They walked to Yvette's office and looked in but it was empty. They turned around and walked to her bedroom door and knocked but nobody answered. They knocked again only louder still no answer but they could hear faint sounds coming from her room. Ernestine opened the door and walked in.

Yvette wasn't in the bed so Ernestine called out "Yvette, honey where are you?" They heard Yvette in the bathroom throwing up. They rushed in the bathroom and found her lying on the bathroom floor gagging. She wasn't actually throwing up it was dry heaves but she couldn't stop. Her face was all red from straining and constant gagging and heaving. Ernestine and the others were down on the floor with Yvette trying to help her up. She wasn't able to move on her own. "Oh my God" Her mother yelled. "Call the ambulance" Lawnyae raced over to the phone and dialed 911. Ernestine yelled to Octavia "Go get Tony" Octavia raced out of the bathroom and down the stairs. She yelled to Kim "Where's Tony?" Kim looked up startled and then worried when she saw the scared look on Octavia's face. "He's in the pool room" "Where is it? Where the hell is it?" Kim shrugged her shoulders "I don't know exactly. Kim pointed to the wall "The intercom" Octavia ran over to the wall where the white box was. "How do you use this?" Kim read the directions on the side of the buttons. "It says to push #68 for the poolroom then speak into the speaker" Octavia followed the directions. She yelled into the speakers "Tony come upstairs something's wrong with Yvette" Tony was just about to make his winning shot when he heard the loud frantic voice over the intercom. He looked at the intercom then he threw the pool stick down and raced up the stairs. The others followed including Eva. Excitement raced through her veins; she knew exactly what was happening.

Tony came racing out of the basement along with the others. He saw Octavia and Kim standing near the stairs waiting on him. He ran up to Octavia and asked. "What's wrong?" "I don't know we just found her like that!" Octavia said frantically. "Like what?" Tony yelled. Tony raced up the stairs and sprinted down the hall to his bedroom. He burst through the doorway yelling, "Where is she?" "In the bathroom" Octavia yelled. Tony ran in the bathroom followed by everybody else. He saw Yvette lying on the floor steady heaving and gagging. With every heave and gag her body jerked. Tony jumped on the floor and grabbed Yvette up in his arms. He was going to pick her up but they all yelled "Leave her down there man" "Did anybody call the ambulance?" Tony asked. "Yeah their on the way" Robin said. Tony held Yvette to him rocking her back and forth. Fear was written all over his face. He rocked her and kissed her forehead; trying to calm her down but nothing helped. They had tried to get her to drink some water in between the spasms but she was unable to. They all stood around watching Tony rock Yvette and rubbing her back trying to quiet the heaves and whispering in her ear. "It's ok baby. It's alright I got you baby. I love you"

Tony looked down at Yvette's face and almost cried. Her face was red and her eyes were rolling back in her head as she continued to gag. He continued to rock her and whisper in her ear "Hold on baby, hold on, I love you sweetie, please hold on for me baby. Relax baby, relax and listen to my voice" He was trying to calm her nerves so that her stomach would stop the spasms, which was causing the dry heaves and gags. When he trained for a fight he caught leg spasms and stomach spasms all the time so he knew he had to try and get her to calm her nerves and try to take deep breaths. The doorbell rang. Kim was closest to the door so she raced downstairs to open the door for the paramedics. She showed them to the bedroom where Yvette was. They rushed in and began asking all kinds of question about her condition. Nobody knew anything. They didn't pump her stomach because the dry heaves was an indicator that her stomach was empty. They put her on a stretcher and rolled her out of the room and down the stairs and out the front door.

Tony grabbed his jacket and keys ran out behind the paramedics. Yvette's mother and sisters followed him. Everybody except for Eva, Mark, Kim and their kids went to the hospital.

Tony helped the nurse hold Yvette's arms as the doctor attempted to put an IV in her arm to get some fluids in her to stop the dry heaves. The doctor succeeded in getting the IV in Yvette's arm. The paramedics were able to get some medicine in her to slow the heaves down a bit but not stop them completely. As the fluids went into Yvette's veins the heaves began to slow down, then they stopped altogether. Tony was able to breathe a sigh of relief when Yvette was able to sleep peacefully without the spasms. He was so afraid for the baby. The doctor had her blood drawn to run some test. Tony sat next to Yvette sponging off her face with a wet sponge the nurse had given him. Her mother and sisters walked in and stood around her bed. Ernestine walked up to Yvette and kissed her on the cheek. She had been crying and praying in the waiting room they all had. Ernestine kissed her again and said "My baby" she whispered in her ear "I love you honey." Yvette was sound asleep she had worn herself out. They all sat silently in her room and waited for the doctor to come back with any news on her condition. They had been sitting in Yvette's room for two hours when Yvette was starting to move around in her sleep. They all waited anxiously for her to wake up but she didn't. The doctor entered the room with his chart. He spoke to them telling them that it looked like Yvette had been poisoned and even though her body had rejected the poison right away the dry heaves and gagging was a side effect of the drug that was used to poison her.

He said he didn't think the baby was harmed but they didn't know for sure so they were going to keep Yvette overnight so they could run some more test on her and the baby. Yvette was admitted into the hospital that night; her family stayed overnight with her including Tony. Only one person was permitted to sleep in her room with her but Tony raised such a stink and asked for a private room for Yvette so they could be alone with her. They told him her insurance wouldn't cover a private room but Tony wrote them a check on the spot for the additional cost and Yvette was moved into a private suite. Her family was able to stay in the room with her and

Tony. They brought up extra cots for them all to sleep on. Yvette didn't wake up through the night. The nurses were in and out of the room taking her temperature and blood pressure and changing her IV bag. It seemed according to the doctor who came in later in the night that because of Yvette's pregnancy she was dehydrated which is what caused the bad reaction to the poison after she had thrown it all up. Around 7 a.m. Yvette was waking up. Her throat was so dry she could hardly talk. Tony called the nurse into the room to examine her. After the nurse examined her she left the room and came back with a cup of ice cubes and a fresh cup of water for her. She poured a cup of water and fed it to her slowly. Yvette tried to swallow but it was hard; eventually she was able to swallow the water. She handed Tony the cup of ice and told him to feed it to her slowly. She raised Yvette's bed so that her head was elevated a bit then she left the room saying she had called the doctor and he would be up shortly. Yvette's lips were dry and chapped and she had dark circles around her eyes and dark vein lines that looked like bruises on her face. The nurse said it was because she had thrown up so much and all of the heaving and gagging caused her to bust the blood vessels in her face. She said it wasn't serious and the bruises would go away as she got stronger. The test the doctor had run on the baby came back that morning that everything was fine and the baby was healthy.

Everyone was able to breathe a sigh of relief. They wanted to keep Yvette for 24 hours to make sure everything was ok with her and the baby. The doctor said by 4:00 p.m. he would release Yvette from the hospital if there were no other complications. Everybody was able to relax once they knew Yvette and the baby were fine. Tony called home and gave his brother Mark the good news. He called his driver to come and pick up Yvette's family and take them back to his house so they could refresh and unwind. Ernestine promised she would come back so Tony could go home and change but Tony declined. He said he wasn't moving until the doctor released Yvette. Yvette still wasn't able to say much but she waved goodbye to her family as she watched them leave.

Yvette felt so sore and weak and tired from her ordeal. She had heard what the doctor said to Tony and her family that the poison did not harm the baby. She knew right off the bat that Eva had poisoned her; in fact as she lay on the floor of the bathroom she knew it was the tea that Eva had given her that caused her to react like that. She was so grateful to God for watching over her and her baby. Eva tried to come against her but God had her back. "Thank You Jesus" Yvette said a silent prayer. She remembered everything Kim had told her about Eva. She looked at Tony wondering if she should mention it. Hell yeah you should mention it to him. This woman tried to kill your baby. Yvette thought to herself.

Yvette took a deep breath and said "Tony I have something to tell you" Tony looked at Yvette with concern on his face. "What is it baby? "When I was working in my office yesterday your mother came in and she gave me a cup of jasmine tea. She said it would soothe my stomach and help with the morning sickness. She sat there and talked with me until I drank all of it. In fact she made sure I drank all of it. As soon as she left that's when I started throwing up and I didn't stop. I believe she was the one who poisoned me" Tony stood up and walked away from Yvette. He stood in front of the window looking out. "Yvette I don't think she would do that; I mean that's her grandson" He said. "But Tony she was the one that gave me that tea and I was fine before I drank it. Yes I was feeling my usual queasiness but no more than usual. And when have you ever seen me doing what I was doing yesterday." Tony turned and looked at Yvette. "I don't think my mother poisoned you Yvette. She wouldn't do that. The doctor said you were dehydrated and that's why you were throwing up like that" "He also said that my body had rejected the poison. Who would poison me Tony? Surely you don't think my family did it. It's no secret that your mother doesn't like me. The way she's been treating me since she got here" Tony was starting to get frustrated with Yvette. "Baby you don't know what you're saying. My mother couldn't possibly do something like that. Even if she doesn't like you why would she try and kill her grandchild?" Yvette paused. "Tony ask yourself this question who would poison me? Before your mother came to our home this had never happened" Tony turned around and faced Yvette.

"Look Yvette now I know my mother came off a little rude when she first got here but that's no reason for you to blame her of poisoning you. That's a serious accusation." He said. "So what do we do now Tony? Do we question the people in our home about their whereabouts or do we just chalk this up to an accident? I don't know many people who accidently poison themselves." She said. Tony paused, "Well are we just going to let it go?" She said. "I don't know Yvette what do you propose we do?" He said. "For one you can question your mother about this," She said. "Why would I go and accuse my mother of something I know she didn't do. You talking crazy now, shit. How about I question your damn mother?" He said. Yvette looked at Tony like he was crazy. "You don't have to get mad Tony. Why don't we just drop this right now?' She said. "Yeah let's drop it.' Tony picked up his keys and grabbed his jacket and walked out of the hospital room. Yvette watched him go. Tears began to sting her eyes and fall down her face as she lay in the hospital bed.

By 6 p.m. that evening Yvette had been released from the hospital. The doctor had sent her home with medication for her morning sickness and told her to take it easy for the next few days. He also told her to follow up with her gynecologist the next day. He told her the poison was completely gone out of her system and the baby was healthy and doing just fine. Yvette asked what kind of poison it was he said that it was a rare kind of plant that grows in South America usually comes in powder form and used to cause abortions. He said it would be hard to find in America, so whoever did it, probably had the drug on them already or they keep a supply of it. Yvette didn't mention this information to Tony when he came back to pick her up. Her mother had come back to the hospital and she had told her what she told Tony about his mother. She asked her to keep it to herself and not tell her sisters because she didn't want them to confront Tony or his mother it would only make matters worse.

Tony was waiting in his car in front of the hospital door. He stepped out of the car when he saw the nurse and Yvette's mother exit the hospital. The nurse pushed Yvette to the car and Tony opened the door and helped the nurse get Yvette in car. He put her balloons and plants in the trunk. Yvette's mother got in the backseat and they pulled away. Tony hadn't said much to Yvette since he had come back to pick her up. When he left the hospital that morning he didn't return nor did he call her. He had come back to the hospital around 4:30 p.m. thinking she would have been released. Yvette hadn't said much to Tony either. Tony pulled up in front of the house and got out the car and came around to open Yvette's door. He helped her out. Yvette still felt a little weak but she was able to walk. Tony held her upper arm to support her so she wouldn't fall. As they walked through the front door Kim and Robin were in the front sitting room talking. Robin jumped up when she saw Yvette and rushed forward to hug her and Kim followed her. Everyone else came in and greeted Yvette with hugs. Yvette walked over to the couch and sat down. Tony went back to the car to get her things.

Tony walked past the ladies as he carried Yvette's things upstairs. He placed them in their bedroom. He turned the sheets down on the bed so that Yvette could get some rest when she came upstairs. He thought about what she said about his mother and what the doctor said about the poison. Tony didn't want to believe that his mother had poisoned his fiancée and put her own grandchild in danger. Yvette must have gotten a hold to something or ate something that may have had the poison in it. But even as he thought that he knew it was farfetched. But he still refused to believe his mother would be capable of hurting her own flesh and blood. He knew his mother despised Yvette to be honest he had expected as much. Eva was very hard on the women he'd chosen to be with. Which is why he hadn't told her Yvette was pregnant. In fact he didn't even want to invite her for Christmas but she had heard that he was living with a woman and she wanted to check her out. But he knew the only women she approved of were women from their island.

Eva had betrothed Tony to Eleshia when they were only eight years old. Tony was supposed to marry her after he graduated college and got a job but he dropped out of college and got into boxing and he never went back. After he started winning fights and then became the champ he forgot all about his being betrothed to Eleshia in fact he never wanted to marry Eleshia. The truth is he never loved her but he was too afraid of his mother to tell her he didn't want to marry the woman she'd chosen for him. On their island a man who's betrothed to a woman can only marry her if he can take care of her. Tony got so caught up in the lifestyle he was living and the American women he was dating that he never went back for her. Eva was mad at him for that and therefore was against her sons marrying or dating American women. Tony sat down on the bed with his elbows resting on his leg he dropped his head in his hands out of frustration. I'll be glad when everybody is gone home. Two more days Tony, just more days. Tony said to himself.

Tony looked up when he heard Yvette and her mother coming down the hall. He stood up and waited for them to enter the room. Yvette's mother held her under her arm as she walked slowly in the room. Despite her protest that she could walk on her own her mother still insisted on helping her. Yvette stomach muscles were sore but other than that she was fine. She was still having morning sickness despite the medicine the doctor had given her. All she wanted to do was lie down and sleep for a little while. As Yvette approached the bed she and Tony held eye contact. She could tell he was still upset with her. Yvette wasn't worried about that she was concerned with getting herself well for the Divas big New Year Eve ball. She had two days to get well enough to attend.

She paused in front of the bed and she sat down slowly. Tony grabbed her arm to steady her. "Do you need help undressing?" Yvette looked up at Tony before she spoke "No I think I can manage it." Yvette got up and walked to her closet and began to take her clothes off. When she came out of the closet she expected Tony to be gone but he and her mother were still standing next to the bed. Yvette got in the bed and Tony pulled the covers over her. He kissed her forehead and asked if she needed anything. "No I think I'm ok for now. Thanks." Tony nodded and left the room. Ernestine sat down next to her daughter. "How do you feel?" She asked. "I feel a little sleepy and sore," Yvette said. "Well unfortunately sweetie you can't take any pain medicine," Her mother said. "I know" Yvette responded. "Well I'm gone let you sleep. Do you want me to turn the TV on before I leave?" Ernestine asked. "Yeah that's fine." Ernestine grabbed the remote and turned the TV on. She kissed her daughter on the head and left the room and closed the door behind her. Yvette sat up in the bed and massaged her temples in a circular motion. She looked over at the table and grabbed her cell phone. She knew Krystal and Tonya both were due home today. She wondered if they had landed. Yvette dialed Krystal's cell number. She got no answer then she tried Tonya and got the same response. She put her phone down and scooted down in the bed and pulled the covers over her. She picked up the remote and started surfing through channels. She couldn't find anything interesting so she turned to Lifetime channel and watched it until she fell asleep.

Hours later Yvette awoke to the sound of Krystal's voice saying softly "Wake up sleepy head" She opened her eyes and saw Krystal standing over her. Krystal sat down on the bed next to Yvette. Yvette sat up wiping her eyes. Krystal reached over and hugged Yvette and Yvette hugged her back. Krystal tucked a strand of stray hair behind Yvette's ear that was dangling in her face. She said softly "I heard what happened" "How did you find out?" Yvette asked. "Well I called your cell several times when I landed but you didn't answer so I called the house phone and I talked to Tony. Girl I was so worried when he told me you had to spend the night in the hospital so I rushed right over here." Krystal said. "Aw Krissy you didn't have to do that. I'm fine girl." Yvette said weakly. "I know but you my girl you know I had to check on you. Plus I wanted to give you the things I bought for the baby. I was so anxious to give them to you that's why I was blowing your phone up. You wanna see em?" Krystal asked. Yvette smiled "I can't believe you buying stuff already." She said. "Girl I couldn't resist." Krystal reached down and grabbed the four bags of baby gifts and handed them to Yvette. Yvette shifted to make herself more comfortable in the bed. As she moved she winced in pain and moaned a bit. Krystal frowned and looked at Yvette

"What's wrong?" "My stomach is still a little sore." Yvette said. Now Krystal was confused. "Why would your stomach be sore?" She asked. "From excessive vomiting." Yvette said. "When did that happen?" Krystal asked. Yvette looked at Krystal confused. "Yesterday evening. I thought you said Tony told you what happened?" She said. "Tony just said you had spent the night in the hospital because you weren't feeling well." Krystal responded. "Girl Tony didn't tell you the full story." "What's the full story? "Well it all started yesterday afternoon when I was in my office working" Yvette said. She went through the whole thing with Krystal.

Krystal frowned and said, "So how do you know it was her?"

"Krystal, are you serious? She hates me she's made it perfectly clear from the beginning that she doesn't approve of me." Yvette said. "Well did you mention this to Tony?" She asked. "Yes I did and he doesn't believe his mother would harm her own grandchild" Yvette said. "Well he has a point Yvette why would she want to harm her own grandchild?" Yvette was getting frustrated with Krystal.

"Well before she came in my office yesterday Kim, Tony's Sister in Law came up and told me not to let Eva get to me. She told me she didn't like American women and she said she tried come between her and Mark when they were first married" She said Eva stressed her out so bad she lost her first baby" Yvette said. Krystal's raised her eyebrow at that bit of information. "So you think maybe she poisoned Kim to? "That's exactly what I think." Krystal sat silent for a minute just thinking then she responded. "It does seem kind of strange how she offered you the tea and had never spoken to you up until that point" "This is what I'm saying." Yvette said. Krystal was starting to get mad. "Where is this Eva I want to meet her?" Krystal said. "I don't know I haven't seen her." Yvette said. "So what did the doctor say?" Krystal asked. "The doctor said my body rejected the poison right away which is why I was vomiting like I was. After all the fluids were out of my stomach I was just gagging and dry heaving, I don't know how long. The doctor said the cause of that dry heaves was dehydration." "The doctor actually said you had been poisoned?" Krystal asked. "YES girl!" "And who does Tony think poisoned you?" Krystal asked. "I don't know he never said he just don't believe it was his mother." Yvette said. "Surely he's not suggesting your family would do it?" Krystal said. "He said maybe it was my nosey mother but I think he just said that out of anger." Yvette responded.

"Girl that was nothing but God that kept anything from happening to you and that baby" "I know I thank God for his favor over us. Now Tony's mad at me he hasn't said much to me since I confronted him in the hospital about this." Yvette said, "Well he has to get to the bottom of this. It's not like it happened in a restaurant or something this happened in his home and intentionally." Krystal said. "I know but when it comes to his mother according to Kim he and his brother are blind where she is concerned; she can do no wrong in their eyes." Yvette responded. "Well they better wake up and soon because this is bullshit." Krystal said. Yvette knew Krystal was upset because she hardly ever cursed. "I'll just be glad when they leave." Yvette said. "When are they leaving? Krystal asked. "The day after The Diva Ball." Yvette said. "Yvette until then you watch your back." Krystal warned. "I know I am. My mother said she'll prepare all of my meals from now on and she said she's not leaving until Eva does." Yvette responded. "Good I met your mother downstairs and she looks like she don't play." Krystal said. "She don't when it comes to her kids." Yvette said. "Don't have me and Tonya to have to come over here and stand guard because you know we will." Krystal said. Yvette laughed then held her stomach from the pain.

Krystal watched Yvette thinking she wanted to talk to her about her engagement. She just didn't think he was the one. But she decided against it; she would keep praying that God's will would be done not hers or anyone else's but the Lord's. Krystal visited with Yvette for a while longer. They looked at all of the gifts Krystal had bought from California. Soon Tonya joined them and they related the whole sorted story to her. Tonya had the same reaction that Krystal did to the whole situation. After they discussed Yvette's wretched mother in-law to be they got right to the business of the Diva Ball. Thus far they all had taken care of their end of the business so everything was coming along nicely.

It was after midnight when the girls left. Yvette got up and took a shower and changed her pajamas and decided to go downstairs and see what everybody was doing. As she exited the stairs she headed for the family room. She heard faint whispers and hushed tones. One of the voices she heard she knew was Tony but she didn't know who the other was. She assumed it must be Eva because it was a woman's voice; Yvette creped to the door trying to hear what they were talking about. She got close enough so she could peak through the crack in the door. She saw Tony and he looked angry like he was arguing with somebody. She moved to the side to see if she could see to whom he was talking. It was a woman and it wasn't Eva, this woman Yvette didn't recognize but she had the same island accent as Eva. Yvette strained to hear what they were talking about. Tony looked like he was begging and pleading with this woman. She couldn't hear exactly what he was begging for. Then she heard the voice of the woman and it gave her pause.

Her voice was so familiar to Yvette but she couldn't put her finger on it. She heard the woman say Tony's name and instantly she was reminded of the woman she had heard on the phone yelling out Tony's name when he was in Italy. Could this be the same woman? Yvette strained to see her face. She was dark skinned and she had a pretty face and long hair. In fact she resembled Eva only darker. Maybe that's his sister? Maybe she decided to come after all. Yvette thought to herself. But that theory was quickly tossed out the window when she saw Tony step forward and hold the woman in his arms as if he was comforting her. Yvette had to suppress every urge she had to bust that damn door open and scratch her eyes out. She watched as Tony and this woman kissed and embraced each other like they were lovers. That hurt Yvette worse than any fist to her face or any other part of her body. Suddenly she got the chills and her legs began to get weak. She stood there holding herself as she leaned up against the wall to support her weak legs. Tears began to instantly fall from her eyes. Yvette was about to leave when she bumped into Eva. She had a smug little smile on her face as she said in her island voice "Oh what's the matter dear? Did something upset you?" She asked.

Yvette looked back at the door because she knew Tony had to

have heard his mother say that. And sure enough Tony pulled the door open and looked shocked when he saw Yvette and the tears streaming down her face. He stood there looking at her like he didn't know what to say. Eva had a broad smile on her face now because Eleshia was standing right beside Tony and it was obvious what they were doing because her red lipstick was still on Tony's lips. Yvette had started crying uncontrollably and could not speak to Tony. She was still weak and walked away holding her stomach. Tony watched her go then he looked at his mother. "Why did you let her hear what was going on in here?" He asked. Eva laughed, "I couldn't stop her she was here when I walked up to the door. It's obvious she'd heard what you were talking about because she was crying when I walked up." Tony dropped his head "Shit".

Eleshia spoke up "Tony why are you marrying this woman anyway? You don't love her you love me and you know it." She said. Tony knew he didn't love Eleshia but he didn't want to deny it. He was trying to keep her from making a scene and upsetting Yvette and embarrassing her in front of her family. He knew his mother and Eleshia would cause a scene. Tony loved Yvette and he didn't want to hurt her. He wanted to go after her but he didn't know what to say. Tony turned to Eleshia and said "Leave, go home right now" Eva and Eleshia both frowned at him. "What do you mean go home? I'm here now Tony" she said. "Eleshia go home. You shouldn't have come here anyway." Tony said. "But Eva told me to come she said you wanted to see me" Eleshia said. "I can't deal with this now. I have to go and talk to Yvette." Tony started to walk away but Eleshia grabbed his arm and pulled him back. Tony snatched his arm away and kept walking. He looked back at Eleshia and said, "Go home I mean it. Leave my house now!" Eleshia had tears in her eyes and did as Tony asked. Eva watched in anger. She thought for sure if she got Eleshia there Tony would have a change of heart and want to be with her instead of Yvette. Her plan had failed.

Yvette was in the bathroom lying on the floor holding her stomach crying and vomiting. She had locked the door behind her because she knew Tony would be coming sooner or later. As soon as he entered the room he heard Yvette crying and gagging. He rushed to the bathroom door but it was locked. Tony beat on the door.

"Yvette open up baby" He ran back to the bedroom door and closed it; he didn't want her family to know what had just happened. They were all in the recreation room downstairs. Tony banged on the door again. "Yvette open the door. Let me help you." He said. Yvette felt so horrible as she lay there on the floor crying all she could do was picture Tony kissing that woman with so much love and tenderness. It hurt her heart. And anyone listening could tell she was not crying out of physical pain she was crying from emotional pain. Tony banged and banged on the door but after a while Yvette had tuned him out. All she felt was despair. Maybe it was from years of physical abuse and emotional abuse combined with Tony's betrayal after betrayal. Tony didn't want to break the door down so he sat on the bed and waited for Yvette. It was agony hearing her cry. He just wanted to make sure she was ok. She cried for a while then he heard silence he got up and knocked on the door again. "Yvette can you open the door please" still she didn't answer him. Soon after that he heard the shower and breathed a sigh of relief. She's just taking a shower, He told himself.

Tony waited for Yvette but she was taking a long time so he decided to get his pocketknife and pry the door open. It worked and Tony found Yvette in the shower leaning against the wall with her head down crying silently as the water hit her body. He opened the shower doors and reached for her. She looked up at him with tears in her eyes and sadness. The look of despair he saw in her eyes was enough to make anybody want to cry. She pulled her arm away from him. He tried again to grab her arm but she slapped his hand away. Tony got frustrated and reached in and grabbed her lifting her and carrying her out of the shower and into the bedroom. He threw her on the bed. As soon as Yvette hit the bed she jumped up and ran back into the bathroom. She tried to shut the door behind her but Tony was too fast he was right behind her. He put his arm in the way to block her from closing the door. Yvette grabbed her bath towel and wrapped it around her. As Tony walked towards her again she moved away from him getting ready to run but he caught her up in his arms and carried her back into the bedroom. This time instead of throwing her on the bed he sat down with her on his lap. Yvette tried to get up but he held her tight so she couldn't move. He held her on his lap like a little girl. Yvette gave up the struggle and just sat there.

Tony looked at her trying to find the words to say to her. He didn't know what to say so he just pulled her close to him and laid his head on her chest. Yvette sat there stiff and unmoving.

Finally he spoke and said "Yvette baby I love you so much" Yvette started laughing it wasn't a humorous laugh it was a frustrated laugh. Tony looked up at Yvette in surprise. She continued to laugh waiting for the words to form in her mind that she could yell at him but nothing came. When her laughter had faded she shook her head out of frustration and anger. Finally she said to him "Tony you don't know what love is." She shoved his arms from around her and got off of his lap. Yvette picked up the towel that had fallen when she got up. She began drying off; rubbing her skin roughly out of anger. Then she walked in her closet and started to get dress for bed. Yvette was shoving her clothes on roughly as Tony stood in the doorway watching her. He had never seen Yvette like this before. She shoved pass him and walked over to the bed and sat down. Tony sat down next to her. Yvette looked at him in anger and said, "Leave me alone. I don't have anything to say to you." Tears stung her eyes as they spilled over and ran down her face. Tony lifted his hand and caught the tears with his finger. "Baby don't cry I hate it when you cry." He said.

Yvette slapped his hand away from her face and yelled "You no good selfish son of bitch. You hate it when I cry but it seems you are always behind every tear that falls from my eyes. You have no conscious. You continually hurt me over and over again. I can't take it anymore Tony I can't. You don't know what love is." She said. "Baby I love you. I know I love you. I'm sorry that I hurt you but I love you and I want you to be my wife. I've known that from the first moment I laid eyes on you that night at the club. I knew I wanted you in my life for a long time to come. I don't know why, I...the other women it's just something I've always done. You don't know what it's like baby. When you have money and fame, women throw themselves at you all the time. You wouldn't believe some of the things they do to be with me. But I've always told them all that I have a woman and I wasn't looking for a replacement. I let them know up front that I love my woman and she's not going anywhere." Tony said. Yvette laughed, "I guess I should feel privileged that my man or my fiancé let his other women know that I'm number one in his life. I bet they get a good laugh out of that one." Tony stood up and yelled, "What the hell do you mean by that? "What the hell do you think I mean by that," Yvette exclaimed. "You telling the women that you running up in that you love me and I'm number one. If that were true you wouldn't be messing around with them." Yvette said.

"Yvette you not a man you don't understand that statement. Any man would understand that. It means you love your wife or your woman but the other women are just those other women. You don't have any emotional attachment to them it is just sex. Men understand that concept." He said. "I guess they do since they're the ones who invented it." She said. "It's not like that. It's an honor when a man tells another woman that he has a woman who he loves and she's number one in his life. Women understand that." Tony said. "Well I'm a woman and I definitely don't understand it." She said. "I don't mean you, I mean the kind of women who mess with another woman's man. They don't have any morals they'll do and say anything to get with a brother with money." Tony said. "Tony I'm a woman and let me tell you this; when a man is willing to cheat on his wife or girlfriend and he tells the other woman I love my wife. Do you know what women hear? Women hear and see a man who seems unhappy in his relationship and if he came looking for me then maybe I can take him from her. There's a chance for us. That's all they think regardless to what you tell them. You wanna know why you have trouble getting rid of the women after you through with them. It's because women associate sex with love and we become attached to the men we sleep with" She said. Tony stared at Yvette. "There is just no way Tony that women can play this game that men invented without forming emotional attachments to them. It's not the way we're wired. What I saw tonight Tony when you kissed that woman is that you love her," Yvette said. Tony stood there silent.

Yvette's bottom lip started to quiver as she realized he wasn't even going to deny it. "Tony" Yvette said. Tony looked at Yvette then responded. "I love you baby." Tears ran down her face because she realized that he was just saying that to make her feel better. All this time she believed he loved her and only her because that's what he had been telling her for years. "Tony you are lying to me. You don't love me you love her. Don't you? She said. "Yvette, don't be silly baby I love you." He said. "Why are you marrying me? It's her you love." Suddenly she realized something. "You only marrying me because I'm pregnant aren't you?" Yvette asked. Tony walked towards Yvette and he reached out and grabbed her by the arms and pulled her into his embrace. He hugged her even though she struggled to get free. She couldn't break free of Tony's embrace so she gave in to the feel of his big strong arms wrapped around her. She wanted to believe she was wrong about him. Tony hugged and rocked Yvette.

When he felt she was calm he let her go and sat her down on the bed and said to her. "Yvette it's you I love. I've known Eleshia all of my life and yes I used to have a physical relationship with her and I once cared for her but since you've been in my life you are everything to me, Yvette." Tony said. Yvette listened he seemed sincere. At that moment she had to decide if she was going to believe what she'd seen with her eyes or if she was going to believe what she was hearing from the heart of the man she loved. Yvette laid her head on his shoulders her decision was made. She loved Tony so much and desperately wanted to be his wife. So she did what any woman in love would do she believed her man.

December 31st New Year's Eve Night

After much protesting with Tony and her mother; Yvette convinced them she was well enough to attend the Diva ball. Yvette was finally getting dressed. She wanted to get dressed at the Venue where the ball was being held with her girls but Tony wouldn't hear of it. She sent over Krystal and Tonya's outfits to the venue. Yvette had chosen gold ball gowns for them. They were beautiful and similarly made. Each dress had something unique about it to fit each one of their personalities. For Tonya hers was a short gold halter dress with sequins. Tonya had the short haircut and nice legs to pull that off as well as the personality; she was sassy. For Krystal her gown was a little more classy but sexy. Her gown was gold with sequins but it was long with a long split up the back and had one sleeve. Yvette's gown was a strapless, long, gold sequin dress with a split on each side. Yvette wore gold stilettos sandals with a strap around the ankle. Tonya wore gold wrap around the leg stiletto sandals and Krystal wore gold stilettos that looked similar to a boot but they were sandals. Krystal wore her hair long and straight and Yvette wore the long curly look and it really suited her and of course Tonya was rocking her short and sexy bob. Yvette had done a great job with the wardrobe.

They wanted to be known as a classy trio like EnVogue but with one less girl and they were well on their way of becoming just that. When Yvette was finished getting dressed, she headed downstairs where the others were waiting for her. It had taken Yvette a little longer to get dressed because she had to stop in between to sit down or lie down because of the queasiness she was feeling. Yvette was getting quite tired of the morning sickness. She wondered why the hell it was called morning sickness. It should be called morning, noon and night sickness. She had been popping saltines crackers all evening in an effort to stop her nausea. When she descended the stairs everyone was waiting for her in the living room. Tony had arranged for two limos to take them all to the Venue. He had hired babysitters for the evening for the kids. Tony stepped forward and offered her his arm. She grabbed his arm and allowed him to escort her to the car. Yvette stopped at the closet to get her tan and black mink stole. Tony draped the stole over her shoulders and opened the door. He was wearing a black tuxedo that Yvette had picked for him. Everyone else followed them out of the door and got in the limos. They were on their way. Yvette, Tony and Yvette's mother and Octavia and Mario rode in one of the limo. Kim and Mark along with Robin, Demetrius, Lawnyae and Lester rode in the other limo. Eva decided she didn't want to go so she was spending time with some family and friends that night.

They arrived at the Venue before the event was scheduled to start. Yvette escorted them all in and got them a table in the VIP section. She and Tony went back stage to find Tonya and Krystal. She found them in their dressing room all decked out and ready to go. They greeted each other with a hug and they kicked it back stage until the show started. Yvette was still feeling queasy and uncomfortable but she wouldn't dare say anything because she didn't want Tony and the girls to make her lie down and miss out on all of the fun. A lot of time and planning had gone into tonight's event and Yvette was not about to miss out on the fun. The Divas had lined up two R&B groups and one comedian all three were major headliners. The ball was scheduled after the performance. The curtains would be removed and there would be a dance floor and dinner would be served. There was a five-course meal planned for the evening with coffee and nuts at the end. It was an elaborate affair. They had hired a band to play while they ate and afterwards for dancing. The Diva's Promotions would be known for elegance and style and class after this evening. They knew how to put on a show for any occasion and tonight would prove it. When it was time for the show to start, they headed for the stage entrance where they would be presented. The crowd went wild when they walked out on stage. It was a full house! They warmed up the crowd as they usually did before they announced their first guest.

As the night went on the stars rocked out and brought the house down. Soon it was time to open the curtains and dinner was served. Yvette, Krystal and Tonya joined their friends and family at the VIP tables. Yvette picked and nibbled at her food not wanting to upset her stomach any more than it already was. Boy I sure can't wait until this morning sickness passes, Yvette thought to herself. She looked around the table watching her family and friends enjoy the gourmet food. She envied them all. When dinner was over they were able to mix and mingle with the guests. Champagne and other drinks were being served. Yvette was holding a conversation with the CEO of their radio station. He was congratulating her on a successful evening. He was quite impressed with the Divas and ready to promote them. Their conversation ended and she started to walk away when all of a sudden someone walked up on the side of her and bumped her. Yvette turned without even looking and said "Oh please excuse me" "You excused bitch." When she heard the profanity she turned and looked to see who was calling her out of her name. It was Tamika, the girl from their Christmas Party. Yvette looked her up and down and said, "Excuse me. Did you just call me a bitch?

"Yes you did hear me correctly." Tamika said. Yvette was too much of a lady to get indignant with her in public. "Look I don't know what your problem is but it's not with me." Yvette said. Tamika sucked on her teeth and pointed her finger at Yvette and said, "Yes it is with you. You think you all that cus you got Tony to propose to you. But I'm here to tell you, you ain't nothing. Do you know how many times I done had yo nigga? The only difference between you and me is you got the drop on him before I could, that's all. But I tell you what all that's about to change" Tamika said. Yvette was furious right about now. She wanted to hit Tamika in her face. "What are you talking about?" Yvette asked. Tamika smiled because she knew she had Yvette's attention and now she was going to pour it on thick. "You not the only one carrying his baby" Yvette was starting feel faint. Tony had told her she was not pregnant. Tamika could see she had got the best of Yvette with her information. She pushed even further. "You better talk to the nigga and let him know if he don't square up with me by tonight regarding this baby; I'll be talking to the press right here in yo little fancy party. Ok?" Tamika said. Yvette was on the verge of tears as she walked away from Tamika. Tamika yelled out to Yvette as she walked away. "You betta holla at him." Yvette felt like she was walking around in a daze as she looked for Tony. She spotted him near the bar with a crowd of people laughing and talking. She was only a mere 20 feet from Tony but by the time she had reached him she felt she was going to faint. She walked up to Tony and linked her arm in his.

Tony looked down at Yvette. She looked tired. He looked in her eyes and knew something was wrong. "What's wrong?" he whispered in her ear. Tony led Yvette away from the crowd he was talking with and led her to their table and pulled a chair out for her. He sat down next to her and pulled her chair close asking her again "What's wrong? Do you feel ok? Yvette was getting ready to speak as she held her head up she saw Tamika switching towards them with her ghetto ass. "Oh God hear she comes." Yvette said. "Hear who comes? Before he could even get all of the words out of his mouth he looked up in the direction Yvette was looking in and saw who she was referring to. Tony started to get nervous as she came and sat right down at their table across from them both. She folded her hands and smiled at Tony. "I assume yo little fiancée delivered my message." Tamika said. "What message? "Oh wifey to be, you didn't tell him?" Tamika laughed, this night was getting better and better. She was more than happy to deliver the message herself. "Oh since she didn't have the balls to tell you like a real bitch I'll tell you myself. That's what I get from sending a weak, sorry, scary no rhythm in the bed having hoe to the job for me." She was looking at Yvette as she said each word. "What the hell are you talking about Tamika?

She smiled and said "Like I told wifey to be here. You have 'til before midnight to square me away concerning this baby or else I'll be speaking to the press right here tonight." Tony looked at Tamika with murder in his eyes. "What do you want Tamika?" Tears fell from Yvette's eyes as she saw he was not even going to deny it. He was having a baby with this woman. The pain she felt was like a blow to the chest. Tamika and Tony continued to conduct business right in front of her like she didn't even exist. Usually Tony would be apologizing and swearing he was innocent but not tonight because there was the threat of his reputation on the line. "I want $10,000 a month in child support starting tonight. I want a car to drive and I want you to put my name on the condo." They share a condo together? Yvette thought to herself. Tony spoke in a calm exact voice when he said "First of all I'll be establishing paternity because you ain't getting a dime from me if that is not my seed you carrying if you are carrying anything. Secondly you are not going to dictate a damn thing to me. I'll give you what I think you should have and not a dime more. And if you wanna pull this little stunt with the press I strongly advise you to think again. You wanna play games with me you better be prepared to pay the price." Tamika actually appeared scared at Tony's threat to her.

Yvette sat there trying to make some sense out of what was happening to her. Again she asked herself, how did I get here? Yvette felt light headed she dropped her head in her hand. Tamika had gotten up and left after Tony's threat. Tony looked down at Yvette for a moment then he asked, "Are you ok?" She looked up at him and his expression was hard and unforgiving. He didn't even seem concerned like he usually was. He was just hard and cold even to her. "I need to go to the back can you walk me? Tony stood up and helped Yvette to her feet and steadied her with his arm around her waist as he walked her slowly to the backstage area where they could have some privacy. Tony sat Yvette down in a chair in the Diva's dressing room. He walked in to the bathroom and wet a napkin and placed it on Yvette's head. Yvette closed her eyes as the cool wet napkin soothed her, resting her head on the back of the chair. Tony stood there watching her. Yvette opened her eyes and looked up at him waiting for him to say something; to beg and plead like he usually did but tonight there was none of that from Tony. It was a side of him she was not familiar with and it scared her, because it reminded her of how Leonard had gotten after so many times catching him cheating it was as if he was tired of putting on fronts.

It took her to a place she knew she didn't want to be ever again. Yvette removed the wet napkin from her forehead. She didn't know what to say but she knew what she had to do. There was no way she was going to stick around and end up in the same marriage she had escaped from. She loved Tony but she didn't want to experience that kind of pain ever again from a man. Tony must have sensed what she was feeling because his expression started to soften and he began the theatrics he normally performed. "Baby I know that was hard for you to see and hear but I couldn't help it. I can't afford a scandal attached to my name right now. With our wedding and the baby I don't want to do that to you or our unborn child. I hope you can forgive me. This thing with her happened a long time ago. I don't even think the baby is mine." Yvette laughed, "Funny, it didn't sound like that to me. And just how pregnant is she Tony? Because her stomach looks as flat as mine." She said. "Baby that's what I'm talking about she's lying." "When was the last time you were with her? Tony frowned and shrugged his shoulders "I don't know maybe a few months ago; six months ago." He cleaned it up knowing a few months ago would make her as pregnant as Yvette is. "Well which one is it?" Yvette asked. "Six months ago baby. I told you it's not mine." "You sound so sure while you're talking to me but when you were talking to her, you didn't sound very sure. You sounded like maybe quite possibly the baby is yours." "Look Yvette we got guest out here. I'm not about to get into this with you. Are you ok?" "Hell Naw, I'm not ok Tony. What do you think? I'm distraught that my fiancée has another baby on the way. And what you mean you not gon' get into this with me. I don't see how you gon' avoid getting into this with me Tony." Tony got frustrated with Yvette. He threw his hands up and walked out of the room leaving Yvette staring at a closed door. She quivered from anger as tears fell down her face. She couldn't believe he walked away from her like that. Yvette didn't even recognize this man she was seeing tonight.

Yvette sat in the dressing room for an hour trying to get her emotions under control. She was still crying when Krystal and Tonya walked in. "What's wrong sweetie?" Krystal rushed to her side. Yvette dried her eyes with a tissue. Tonya and Krystal sat surrounding her. "Tony" is all she could get out. Now that Krystal and Tonya were there her tears seemed to have taken on a mind of their own because she cried harder. They hugged her and comforted her and tried to get her to calm down enough to tell them what had happened. Finally Yvette had a grip on herself. "Tell us what happened boo" Tonya said. Yvette told them only bits and pieces of the story but bottom line she told them she had a fight with Tony. She looked exhausted and tired and fed up. They heard the crowd counting down it was New Years. As everyone on the floor rang in the New Year Yvette, Krystal and Tonya sat back stage holding each other's hands in a circle and praying in 2008.

Los Angeles

As the clock struck midnight Marissa was calling out Curtis's name as they went at it in the hotel room of the Beverly Wilshire. They both had attended a very star studded New Year's Eve party there. Curtis couldn't keep his eyes off of Marissa as she walked around the party flirting with just about every man in the place. It didn't make Curtis jealous but it had been a minute since he had sex so he was very horny and since he was familiar with her, he didn't object when she whispered in his ear her room number and slipped her key in his pocket. He watched her as she made her way out of the ballroom and headed for her hotel room. Curtis followed her a while later.

When he entered the room Marissa was all ready for him. It didn't take long for them to get right down to business. At 1 am Marissa was snuggled up close to Curtis. Curtis lay there looking at the ceiling thinking. He always hated this part of sleeping with Marissa. It made him feel like he had just sinned or made a deal with the devil. He knew it wasn't right but he couldn't help himself where she was concerned. He knew he still loved her but he also knew she was no good for him. A part of him wished things were different between them but the other part wished he could get over her and get on with his life. Although he had been with many women, Curtis still had never met anyone who touched him like Marissa did. Images of Tony's beautiful woman crept into his mind. He really couldn't say that she touched his life because he didn't know her but her face, those lips that body, stuck in his mind.

Sometimes when he was down and depressed he allowed his mind to picture her; he remembered how she felt in his arms. It just felt right to hold her like that, like she belonged to him. Curtis looked at the clock it was time for him to go. He sat up and moved the covers off of him and walked to the bathroom. Marissa held on to his arm to keep him in the bed with her but he pulled away from her and continued to walk to the bathroom. Inside the bathroom Curtis stared at himself in the mirror. "You weak man," he said to himself. He turned the shower on and got in. Curtis scrubbed his skin hard trying to wash away the filth of the sin he allowed himself to be lured into. Marissa was like a bad habit he knew he needed to kick but couldn't. Each time he told himself he would be stronger next time; he wouldn't allow himself to fall so easily. But just like a drug she was hard to kick. The water ran down from his baldhead into his face as he stood under the shower. He took a deep breath and turned the water off. Curtis hurried and dried off so he could get the hell out of that room and get home. He needed to be away from her.

As he was walking out of the door Marissa ran up to him and placed her hands on either side of his face and reached up on her tip toes and kissed him passionately. He should have pushed her away and kept walking but he couldn't. Curtis accepted her tender kiss. It was like she was sealing the deal for next time or just letting him know although he was leaving he was not getting away from her. That kiss almost promised there would be a next time and he knew it. Curtis stood in the elevator as it rode down each floor. "That's the hold she has on me. I couldn't resist her kiss. But this time I got the drop on her cause there won't be a next time for us." He vowed to himself. He wasn't even sure he believed that as he walked off the elevator and headed for the door. He waited outside for the valet to drive his car around. Then he jumped in it and rode home. It was now past 2 a.m. and he wondered how his little sister was doing and how her party went. It was 5 a.m. in Atlanta and Krystal was just leaving the venue. He put his cell in the holder and pressed the loudspeaker button on the cell so he could talk and drive.

"Hello" Curtis heard Krystal's voice and a lot of noise in the background. "Hey Happy New Year baby girl. Where are you?" "Hi Curtis Happy New Year to you to. I'm just leaving the Venue." She said. "Oh yeah how was it tonight? He asked. "Oh it was beautiful we had a great turnout." She said. "Good" He said. "What did you do tonight?" She asked. "Oh I had this New Year's Eve event to go to tonight at the Beverly Wiltshire. It was nice." He said. "Good I'm glad you enjoyed yourself." "Are you driving?" She asked. "Yeah" He responded. "Are you drunk?" She asked. "Naw I'm good. What about you? Are you ok to drive?" Curtis said. Krystal laughed, "Yes I'm fine and I'm not driving. We rented limos for the night." She said. "Where are you heading now?" He asked. "Oh I'm going home. It was a long night and I'm exhausted." She said. "Good that's where you should be. It's too late for a youngin' like yourself to be out running the streets." Curtis laughed. "Oh I ain't even mad at you cause you right." Krystal said. "Well a'ight then you be careful out there and get yo butt in the house. I'll holla at you later. Peace out, I love you." He said. "Peace big bro and I love you too." They ended the call. Curtis looked at his watch. He was tempted to stop and grab a bite to eat before he headed home. He knew Jonathan and his wife were most definitely in for the night and he really didn't feel like eating alone so he decided to head home. His son had spent the night with his mother and Ashley attended a New Year's Eve party with some of her old friends from high school; she would be spending the night out with them. He really didn't have anyone to go home to.

Curtis walked through the front door and disarmed his alarm system, then tossed his keys on the side table by the door. He looked around his big beautiful house. He had everything but happiness. He walked slowly up the stairs to his bedroom to change out of his clothes. He slid into some comfortable lounging pants and a tee shirt and headed down stairs to pour him a drink. He sat in the family room with the remote in his hand flipping through channels, not really looking for anything in particular he was just bored and restless. Finally he locked in the sports channel and attempted to watch the program but his mind began to wander. Curtis started to think about his future, about the New Year and what it would hold for him. He thought about Marissa. He knew if he would allow it she would come back to him. I feel that every time I lay down with her something inside of me objects strongly against her or the act itself. I don't know but I need to just leave her ass along and move on. Curtis thought to himself. I need a woman who's totally committed to me; somebody I can come home to who I can trust when I'm on the road. He thought to himself. Soon he drifted off to sleep. When he opened his eyes it was daylight. Curtis looked at his watch it was 8:00 a.m., he turned the TV off and went upstairs to his bedroom, pulled the covers back and climbed in the bed. He slept for another two hours.

He awoke to soft tender kisses to his face and neck. Curtis knew those soft lips only too well; they belonged to Marissa. "Wake up sleepy head" Curtis turned over to find Marissa lying next to him on the bed. "How did you get in here?" Marissa smiled, "Ashley let me in" "What time is it? "It's time for you to get up." Marissa pulled the covers off Curtis. He snatched them away from her. "Marissa what do you want?" She sat down next to him on the bed and touched his face tenderly "I thought we had a good time last night and I just wanted to spend some time with you." Curtis got up and walked to the bathroom and Marissa followed him in there. "You should have called first Marissa. What if I had been up here with somebody? How would it look for my ex-wife to come barging in my bedroom?" Marissa poked out her bottom lip like a child does when their upset and said "I'm sorry don't be mad at me baby. Besides I did call but you didn't answer." "What does that tell you Marissa? You came over anyway?" "Well I was outside when I called and then Ashley pulled up so I came in with her. Aren't you glad to see me?" Curtis rolled his eyes at her. "Does it look like I'm glad to see you?" Marissa looked down at his erection and smiled. She walked up to him and put her hands on his penis. He slapped her hand away and walked out of the bathroom. He walked into his closet and turned the light on. Marissa was right behind him. She was starting to get a little annoyed with the way he was treating her. "Marissa go downstairs I'll be down there when I get dressed." She tried to seduce Curtis but he didn't allow her to. "Get out of my room Marissa" Curtis yelled at her. Marissa walked out of the room fuming at him.

Los Angeles February 15th 2008

Curtis and Jonathan sat in the meeting room at Agape with their lawyers. They were waiting on their new group and their manager to arrive. They were discussing the contract to ensure everything was in place. The secretary spoke over the speakerphone to let Curtis know his guests had arrived, he told her to show them in. He went back to the business he was discussing with the lawyers. A minute later there was a knock at the door. "Come in," Curtis said. The secretary opened the door and three young ladies walked in with their manager. Curtis and the rest of the men around the table stood up. He greeted them, "Hi you must be Divine" he referenced the group's name. He had never met them; Jonathan had scouted the group when they were on the road and met with their manager. This was Curtis' first time meeting the trio and their beautiful manager.

After Jonathan made the introductions he shook all three of their hands. Then he introduced him to their manager. "Curtis this is Sherry Holmes" He shook her hand "It's nice to meet you Sherry" She smiled seductively and said "It's nice to meet you to Curtis but please call me Strawberry" Curtis smiled he liked her name and knew what it implied. "That's a unique name." "I'm a unique person," she smiled and walked over and took a seat next to her girls. Curtis watched as she walked past him. She was fine she had long red hair and looked like she was bi-racial. She was a little smaller than he preferred his women to be but she was still a 'dime piece'. He was looking forward to working closely with her. As the meeting went on he didn't miss the little smiles and looks she gave him on the sly while nobody else was looking. Oh yeah she want a piece of me, Curtis thought to himself. When the meeting was over and the contracts was signed he and Strawberry exchanged numbers. After the group left, the attorneys departed and Jonathan and Curtis were alone. Jonathan smiled as he looked at Curtis.

"What" Jonathan shook his head and said "Man you are a glutton for punishment" Curtis laughed and said, "What is that supposed to mean? "You go for the same woman every time man." "She's fine" Curtis said. Jonathan laughed, "Yeah I know that's what I mean. She has trouble written all over her." "How can you see that.

I didn't see that" Curtis said. "I know man you never do. Then when you get the decent women you don't hang on to them. It's almost like you sabotage the relationship on purpose when you're with a good woman either that or you let Marissa do it. What's wrong with you?" Jonathan said. Curtis laughed, "Jonathan man you tripping. I don't sabotage anything it just don't work out." Curtis said. "Curtis just think about it, what happened with Lisa?" Jonathan said. "What, nothing man she just. I don't know." Curtis said. Jonathan laughed again "You know what happened. Marissa happened and you allowed it to happen and what about Pam? He asked. "Well Pam decided she didn't want to be bothered with me. I had nothing to do with that," He said. "Curtis you had everything to do with that. You can't allow your ex-wife to have so much access in your life if you expect to keep a relationship. No woman is gone put up with that. I think that's why you go for women just like Strawberry. Who would call themselves Strawberry in this industry and expect to be taken seriously?" They both laughed "Yeah you have a point there" He said. "She's probably an ex-stripper or something but anyway her intentions are not the intentions of a decent woman and you know it" Jonathan said. "Man didn't your mother ever tell you; you can't judge a book by its cover?" Curtis said. "In this instance I think I can" Jonathan said.

"She just might surprise you and turn out to be a nice girl" Jonathan laughed and said, "I highly doubt it. But then I don't think that's what you're looking for. As a matter of fact you never go looking for the good women they seem to always find you" Jonathan said. "So what's wrong with that?" Curtis asked. "Nothing but I mean I'm wondering why you seem to always mess it up somehow?" "You blaming me for every failed attempt at a relationship, with a decent woman as you call them?" Curtis said. "Yes I am because it's true" "No it's not it just seems that way to you" Curtis said. "You're living in denial my friend but you know what I'm gon' let you reside there cus you seem to be happy and that's all I want for you bro, is your happiness." Jonathan slapped Curtis on his back "Now I'll see you later I'm going to be late for lunch with my beautiful wife." They slapped hands and gave each other the one shoulder hug like brothers do and Jonathan left the meeting room leaving Curtis alone to ponder what he had said. Curtis looked at the card Strawberry had given him. It was flimsy because the paper was cheap from that he knew she was small time and this was probably a big break for her and the group. He programmed her cell number in his phone and placed her card in his Rolodex. They would definitely be seeing a lot of each other and he was looking forward to it.

Atlanta February 2008

Yvette was in her home office working on the computer. The Diva's Promotion was blowing up and they were getting busier and busier. It was getting to the point where it was hard to juggle their jobs at the station with their business especially for Krystal. Tonya and Yvette did most of the work because they worked fewer hours than she did. Since the New Year's ball they had been discussing more and more about leaving the radio station altogether and working Diva's Promotions full time. Business was good and they were making good money doing what they loved. They could easily handle giving up their day jobs and still having adequate income. They decided to pray about it and let God lead them. Yvette rubbed her stomach she was starving. It was past lunchtime and she was still working hard. She decided to pause and go down stairs to eat. She got on the intercom and spoke to Rosie in the kitchen and asked her to fix her some lunch and to let her know when it was ready.

Yvette stretched and stood up. It seemed her morning sickness was not getting any better. She was still queasy all the time and feeling weak. She rubbed her stomach and thought about Tony. He was not home as usual. Since New Year's he'd been different. He wasn't as affectionate anymore and he was a little colder and bolder about his cheating. He didn't' apologize for it anymore. He didn't go out of his way to cheat in front of her face but his lack of time spent at home when he wasn't out on the road was evidence that he was spending time elsewhere with someone else. Yvette didn't question him about it though. She really didn't know how to handle it; he was still insisting he wanted to marry her and she knew he was definitely happy about the baby. He was still attentive where her pregnancy was concerned and she still loved the hell out of him. Regardless of his faults he was her fiancée and the father of her child. For that reason she'd decided to marry him. She felt that as long as he wasn't hitting her she could put up with anything. Oh and it turned out that Tamika was pregnant. Tony told her it wasn't his. He said she had lost the baby he had heard but Yvette knew he had made her have an abortion.

Then there was still the question of Eleshia who Tony had

kissed in their home that night. He claimed he had no feelings for her romantically but Yvette didn't care what he said his actions spoke louder than his words. She hadn't seen her anymore. She wondered what he had done with her. He probably paid for her to go back to Barbados. He seemed to be good at cleaning up his messes. Now all he needed to do is work on not making the mess in the first place so he wouldn't have anything to clean up and hide. After lunch Yvette was tired so she went to her room and tried to take a nap. She had planned a small dinner party that was taking place later that night. Krystal had finally met a man she felt was worthy of her and had been dating him for a whole month now. Tonight was the first time Yvette and Tonya would get to meet him. Yvette had invited Krystal and her new man over along with Tonya and her thug. She just hoped Tony would be home to join them. She told him about it last week and reminded him about it earlier that morning. She also texted him to remind him to be home by 5pm dinner was at 6:30 p.m. Yvette tossed and turned in the bed trying to find a comfortable position after awhile she was finally able to sleep.

Tony came home about 4:30 p.m. not wanting to hear his fiancé mouth about him being late. She didn't question him anymore about his whereabouts, which was good because he didn't like lying to her, which is why he didn't bother to apologize anymore. But if she so happened to catch him, which she had already caught him talking on the phone to one of his little freaks, he would not deny it. Tony felt she had put up with it so long why would she even complain about it? He didn't understand women who knew their men cheated on them and every time they'd catch them with another woman they would start acting crazy and crying. But they stayed with the man, so why cry about it when you know already what's going on. He told himself he would stop cheating when he said "I do" until that day he felt he had every right to continue to sow his wild oats. He loved Yvette and wanted to build a life with her and their baby but he also wanted his freedom. Tony knew deep down inside that nothing would change after they were married and he had a sneaky suspicion Yvette thought the same.

As long as she was ok with the way things were between them so was he. He stood over her looking at her. She always looked so innocent and sweet when she was asleep; so precious. Maybe that's what he first saw in her when he first laid eyes on her. That innocent quality, made him want to protect her and keep her all to himself, like putting her away on a shelf just so he could look at her. He liked coming home to her. After doing all his dirt she was like the one thing that was still pure and sweet in his life. Yvette was everything he wanted in a wife. Even Eleshia didn't have the quality Yvette had which is why he never really wanted to marry her. She was just like his mother so controlling and vindictive. He bent and kissed Yvette on the cheek as she slept. She didn't' even stir when he kissed her. She must be tired, Tony thought to himself because Yvette was a very light sleeper. Whenever he would come home and find her sleeping he would kiss her on the forehead or her cheek and she would always wake up. Tony went into the bathroom to shower for the event of the evening.

He really didn't want to be a part of the dinner party. Krystal and Tonya had hated him since the night of the New Year's Eve ball and he didn't want to have to sit at a table with them and endure their glares. But they were Yvette's best friends so he had to make the best of it. One thing he appreciated about them is they never pushed her into leaving him. They offered their love, support and comfort and that's why he never had to convince Yvette not to hang out with them. He liked women who minded their own business. But the minute they get out of control they asses are out of here, he told himself. Tony would make sure of it. He knew Yvette loved him and all he had to do is make a suggestion about her spending less time with them and it was a done deal. He finished showering and walked out the bathroom. Yvette wasn't in the bed when he came out. He wondered where she was. Tony walked over to their walk-in closet but she wasn't there. He assumed she must be downstairs talking to Rosie making sure everything was set for tonight. Tony dried off and got dressed. When Yvette entered the room she saw the closet door opened and knew Tony was in there. She walked on his side of the closet; he was picking out jewelry to wear with his outfit for the night. Yvette walked up and kissed him "Hi baby" He kissed her back grabbing her around her waist and pulling her to him. "What's up sleeping beauty" He said and released her and patted her on the butt. "I'm glad you came home in time for my dinner party. Thank you" Yvette said. "No sweat baby. I told you I would be here didn't I?" He said. Yvette smiled "You did." Tony held out his arm, "Can you put this watch on for me please?" "Sure I can." As she placed the watch on Tony's wrist she was dying to ask him where he had been. She told herself she was not going to ask him. She had gone all this time without prying into his whereabouts and she wanted to keep it that way. Her silence was a telltale sign of what was coming Tony knew that. He was just hoping she wouldn't go there. He didn't feel like arguing with her this evening.

Yvette finished clasping his watch for him. "Thank you baby" He leaned down and kissed her on the lips and turned and walked out of the closet. Yvette followed him. Tony rolled his eyes as he felt Yvette right on his heels. He turned to her and said "Shouldn't you be getting ready baby? "Oh I'm about to" She said. She looked at Tony and he looked at her. Yvette was trying to talk herself out of asking the question she knew would only hurt her feelings. Tony stood there waiting for the inevitable. He held out his hands "Is there something wrong boo? He said. Yvette didn't respond then finally she said "No, nothing. Ima go and get in the shower." Tony nodded his head and turned away. Whew I'm so glad she didn't go there. I really didn't want to be fighting with her this evening. Imagine what kind of dinner party this would have been, Tony thought to himself.

Yvette sat at her vanity stool in her closet putting on her makeup and thinking how close she had come to starting a fight with Tony. I'm really sick of his shit. I know I'm supposed to be used to a man cheating on me so he says but so what; I didn't end a marriage with one lying cheating, violent man to end up in a relationship with a man who may not be beating me with his fist but still hurting me just the same. How can I even consider marrying into some mess like this? Lord, am I that desperate? But he's good to me and I know he loves me. I just love him so much I can't help myself. He said he wouldn't cheat on me after we got married. Why should I believe him? Once a cheat always a cheat; you learned that with Leonard. How many times did he say he wasn't going to cheat anymore and still did it? Yvette told herself. But she knew she didn't have the strength to walk away from Tony not that she wanted to. "Every relationship has its problems. Nobody has a perfect marriage. Why should mine be the exception?" Then out of nowhere Yvette heard that voice in her spirit say "Because beloved you are a child of God. You belong to the highest God. You deserve the best of the best." She knew without a doubt that it was the voice of the Lord speaking to her. She dropped her head because she knew she deserved better. She was just settling for less. Maybe between all the fighting with Leonard and leaving him and meeting Tony; somewhere on this road, I must have gotten tired and gave up. She thought to herself. Lord help me, is all she could think of. She knew she was weak and her spirit was worn down but she knew God would renew her and give her strength to fight if she only called on him for help. She finished getting ready; she didn't want to dwell on her problems; it was Krystal's night and she wanted everything to be delightful and entertaining for her. Krystal was always there for her and she wanted to be there for her tonight.

By 6 p.m. they were all sitting around in the living room talking and laughing. Krystal and Milton sat next to each other on the love seat and Tonya and Otis were sitting on the couch together. Milton seemed to be a very nice man and Krystal really seemed to like him. They looked as if they enjoyed each other's company. Milton was tall about 6'2 and he was as light as Krystal and had a low cut fade. He was a nice looking man; hip and funny. Yvette was happy for Krystal. She needed someone to spend her evenings with. Even though she played tough and acted like being alone didn't bother her, Yvette knew it did. She wasn't unhappy just a little lonely. Tony seemed to get along with Milton and he had already met Otis so everyone seemed comfortable with each other. Around 6:45 p.m. Rosie came in and announced that dinner was ready. They all headed for the dining room. As they were walking to the dining room Krystal got a chance to walk next to Yvette. She linked arms with her and asked, "So what do you think? Yvette smiled and said "Girl I like him. He seems nice." "He is; it's been a long time since I met someone I can actually have a conversation with and whose company I really enjoy." She said. "Girl I'm so happy for you." They entered the dining room and took their seats. Yvette and Tony sat at opposite ends of the table as was customary since they were the hosts. Yvette had Rosie to remove both of the middle pieces from the table to make it smaller for their party of six. During dinner Krystal announced that the

Diva's Promotion would be going out of town to New York to work a job in the first week in March. Yvette and Tonya knew about it but Krystal had to work out all of the details before she announced it. Yvette and Tonya looked at each other excitedly. This would be their first out of town gig and the client they were working for was big on the east coast and had the clout to blow them up big time out there.

Tony looked at Yvette and said "Baby are you sure you gone be able to handle this? Yvette frowned and asked, "Why wouldn't I be able to handle it?" "Well with the pregnancy and the morning sickness and all" He said. "I'll be fine honey," She said. "Ok I just want to make sure." He said. Yvette smiled at Tony more annoyed than anything that he would bring up her pregnancy and insinuate that she couldn't handle it. As if he really wanted her staying behind. Yvette shook her head she knew Tony was genuinely concerned about her. She was just a little cranky and a little tired. She would apologize to him later for being short with him. After dinner they had desert and coffee in the living room and by 10:30 the dinner party was over and their guest were preparing to leave. Yvette kissed and hugged Krystal and Tonya and thanked Milton for coming and Otis and they all left together. Tony had said his goodbyes and headed upstairs. Yvette put the desert dishes and coffee cups in the dishwasher and headed upstairs.

When she got upstairs she paused at their bedroom door not wanting to go inside yet. She decided to try to get some work done in her office so she walked past her bedroom and down the hall and closed the door. The truth is she really didn't want to face Tony alone. It seemed as if they were growing apart. They really didn't talk anymore and Tony always seemed to be preoccupied when he was at home unless of course he wanted to have sex. But he didn't really bother her about sex too much anymore. He knew how painful it was for her and she usually cried every time they were intimate. He would say he would be gentle but he was always rough it seemed. As much as she missed having sex with him she didn't push the issue too much. It bothered her to no end that he was getting his pleasure somewhere else. But there was nothing she could do about it.

Yvette sat in her big black office chair in front of her computer and looked around her office. She didn't have any work to do for Diva Promotions unless Krystal had forwarded her the list of her duties for the New York trip. Knowing Krystal, she probably had, so Yvette logged onto the computer and checked her email and sure enough Krystal had done just that. So Yvette got to work. She had been working for more than an hour when Tony came in. He walked up behind her and kissed her softly on the neck. Yvette leaned her head to one side to invite him to do more. It had been a minute since they had been together so she welcomed his advances. Tony pulled her arm and she got up and they walked to their bedroom.

He rolled off of her breathing hard. Yvette rolled on her side so that he couldn't see her face. Tony turned to look at her "Are you ok? "He asked. Yvette responded "Yes" Tony lay there a while longer then he got up and went into the bathroom to wash up. Yvette sat up in the bed and dropped her head in her hands. She was so disappointed in herself for acting like a baby crying and whimpering during sex. She didn't want Tony running to any other woman because she couldn't take it. Yvette got out of bed and went into the closet and put her robe on; when she came out of the closet Tony was out of the bathroom. She went right in the bathroom without even looking at him.

Yvette turned the shower on and got in. She showered quickly and got out drying herself off. She took her time as she rubbed lotion on her body feeling bad about herself. But then she started to get angry at Tony because she felt he should be patient with her after all she is carrying his baby and she couldn't help the changes in her body. By the time she walked out of her closet she was pissed at Tony and herself; him for being so selfish and her for being so hard on herself. She pulled the covers back on her side of the bed and got in. Tony was already fast asleep. She looked at him for a minute then turned her back on him and lay down. She reached up and turned the lights off and lay in the dark thinking. Finally sleep came but she was still restless. Yvette would surely be tired the next day.

Los Angeles

Curtis sat at a table outside the Apple Pan restaurant with Strawberry eating and talking. They had been seeing each other for weeks now. Curtis was really enjoying spending time with her; she was fun to be with; she was a little ghetto but he didn't mind that because she was unpredictable and the sex was off the chain. As Marissa and her friend Carmen stepped out of the restaurant to choose a table she saw Curtis sitting with some hood rat looking girl. True to form she was not having this; she watched them for a minute. Hmm Curtis really seems to be enjoying himself. I guess I'm going to have to run another one off, Marissa thought to herself. She reached in her purse and pulled out her compact mirror and checked her reflection "Flawless" she said out loud to herself. She said to Carmen, "I'll be right back girl" She got up and started to walk away. "Where are you going? Carmen asked. "To stir things up a bit over here," she pointed in the direction of Curtis. Carmen smiled she didn't even notice him sitting there. "Who is he with?" Carmen said, "I don't know but I'm about to find out" She said. Marissa started to walk away and Carmen said "Girl maybe you should leave them alone. He's not your husband anymore" Marissa looked at Carmen and said, "He'll always be mine." And she walked away. Marissa switched and swayed her way over to Curtis's table. He saw her approaching and stopped in mid-sentence.

Strawberry looked at him then she turned around and saw Marissa walk right past her and up to Curtis. She smiled and said "Hi sweetie" She bent over him and kissed him on the lips. Strawberry sat back and looked them up and down. She couldn't believe the nerve of this woman to come up and kiss her man while she was sitting right there with him. When Marissa came up for air she hugged him around his neck and looked at Strawberry and said "Did you miss me honey?" Curtis removed Marissa's arms from around his neck but by then it was too late. Strawberry was already up and had a hand full of Marissa's hair in her hand. She pulled Marissa up and away from her man. Marissa screamed and she tried to hit Strawberry but she missed. Strawberry had Marissa by the hair and was swinging her to and fro. She pushed her down on the ground and got on top of her and was hitting her; she was yelling and cursing at Marissa as she pounded her. Curtis had jumped up and was trying to get Strawberry to let Marissa go but she had a firm hold on Marissa's hair. It took Curtis and two waiters to pull Strawberry off of Marissa. Carmen had ran over with the intentions of helping Marissa but when she saw how Strawberry was handling her, she decided against it.

When they finally had Strawberry under control Carmen rushed over to Marissa to help her up. Marissa was crying and very embarrassed she wasn't expecting a fight. She thought after she kissed Curtis Strawberry would get up and leave. She had totally missed judged this woman. But Marissa was no punk she looked at Strawberry knowing she would get even with her one way or another. She allowed Carmen to lead her away and they left the restaurant before the police could arrive. Curtis watched them leave he couldn't believe Marissa had actually started this mess. He was pissed at her and he couldn't believe that Strawberry reacted the way she did. He knew she was ghetto but damn this really took the cake.

Needless to say they were asked to leave the restaurant and weren't allowed back there. Curtis was so upset his reputation was on the line. Nothing like this had ever happened to him before. He was yelling at Strawberry when they got in the car. "What the hell did you do that for?" He asked. Strawberry was outraged she looked at Curtis and yelled back "Me what the hell do you mean? Why did you do what you did?" Curtis looked appalled "What the hell did I do? He asked. "You sat your ass there and let that Bitch kiss you right in front of me like I wasn't shit" She yelled. "I didn't tell her to come over there. I didn't even know she was going to be there!" He said. "You didn't try to stop her either did you? I'm from New York and you ain't just gone diss me in front of all those people. That's not how it's gone go down. I did what I had to do. I had to let that bitch know who ever she is that she don't play Strawberry like that ok. And you aint gone play me like that either. I don't know who you use to messing with but I'm not the one to be played with!" Strawberry yelled. Curtis stared at Strawberry because she was definitely not what he was used to. He took a deep breath "You know you right. I should have stopped her and that was very disrespectful to you. I apologize." Strawberry calmed down a bit. She looked at Curtis and said "Well I'm sorry that I reacted the way I did. I'm so use to dirty, grimy people trying to take advantage of me. In New York we act first and ask questions later, so I'm sorry." Strawberry gave Curtis that seductive look and it was on; they drove to a nearby hotel and got one in.

Strawberry watched Curtis get out of bed and walk to the bathroom. She smiled to herself because she thought she was going to lose this one but she was able to hold on to him a while longer. "This negro got money and knows all the right people. I need to hold on to him. But I can see that ex-wife of his is going to be trouble but I ain't worried about that hoe I can handle her; next time I'll have to be slow to anger and not put my hands on her I'm not giving this one up." Curtis washed up in the bathroom looking in the mirror. "This broad is ghetto but damn she got skills in the bed. But this ain't gone last long I can see that. But that's cool cus I can just keep it moving. She might be good to keep on standby though." Curtis thought to himself as he finished washing up. He walked out of the bathroom and Strawberry was standing in the middle of the room looking suspicious. He looked at her and asked, "What's wrong?" She looked at him and said, "Nothing, I was just looking out the window." Curtis looked at his pants on the floor next to her feet. He knew that was not where he had left them but he played it off. I know this trick ain't stealing from me, Curtis thought to himself. He picked up his pants off of the floor. He stared Strawberry straight in her eyes as he put on his pants. He wanted her to know he was not a fool and not the one to be played with. She walked past him and into the bathroom to wash up. In the bathroom Strawberry's heart beat so fast. She thought for sure Curtis had seen her holding his pants and she knew for sure he knew where he had left his pants. She silently cursed herself for being so stupid. I hope I haven't messed things up with him. I can see he didn't believe me; he knew I was checking his pants pockets. But that's ok cus once again I got the drop on that fool. She thought to herself as she smiled at herself in the mirror.

Curtis dropped her off at her apartment and kept going. He needed to stop by Marissa's house to see if she was ok. Strawberry don't play, he was thinking to himself as he reached Marissa's house. He didn't see her car in the driveway so he pulled away. He checked his watch it was still a bit early to head home so he decided to check in on his mother. He hadn't talked to her in a while so he stopped by her house. Delores was sitting on her porch when Curtis pulled up in her driveway. She stood up and smiled "What a wonderful surprise," She said to Curtis as he walked up to the porch. "Come and sit down and have some lemonade with your mother." She poured Curtis a cup of cold lemonade and handed it to him. "It's nice to see you son" Curtis rolled his eyes he knew his mother was being sarcastic because he hadn't seen or spoken with her in a while. "I know it's been a minute mama since I've seen you but I've been busy" Curtis said. "Mmm and what's her name?" Delores asked. Curtis laughed and shook his head. "Mama come on now, I didn't come over here to debate my love life with you. I came to see my favorite girl." He leaned over and kissed her on the cheek.

Delores watched him curiously "What's wrong son?" She said in that mother's knows voice. "Nothing is wrong ma gees can't a son come see his mother without something having to be wrong? Why you acting so suspicious?" Delores turned her head "I've been thinking about you a lot lately son. I don't know why you been on my mind." "Because you love me that's why mama" Delores humph "You not happy Curtis are you? "Mama I'm more than happy I am ecstatic" "Don't lie to me son" Delores pointed her finger in Curtis's chest and said, "You are not happy. Why don't you stop running around here with these less than honorable women and get some help baby?" "Mama, help for what? There is nothing wrong with me" "Son I know you don't like to discuss this but sweetheart if you don't deal with it; it will deal with you and I would rather you get to the bottom of the issue than to have it destroy you baby. You deserve so much more than that. No it was not fair that it happened to you and It is not fair that you had to suffer but baby we go through pain in our life for a reason. What you have to do is get on your knees and ask God what is his purpose for the pain. Then and only then son will you get you're healing. Running around here with all these loose women is not going to serve you well in the end. You just running from your demons and sooner or later you're going to have to stop running and deal with it. Why not now?" She said.

"Mama where is all this coming from?" Curtis asked. Delores shook her head and said "I saw you with that woman with the red hair at the restaurant today. I wouldn't have thought she was your type son. But I saw what happened between her and Marissa. I have to ask you son what are you doing? You allowed Marissa to kiss you in front of that woman and that's why she got that angry and fought her. You could have easily stopped her but you didn't, why?" Delores asked. Curtis looked down in his glass of lemonade. "I didn't know Marissa was gone be there" Delores gave Curtis that warning look and he said "Mama it's complicated I can't explain it to you" "Can you explain it to yourself?" She asked. "Of course I can" "Then you can explain it to me. I know you don't owe me any explanation but I want to know what's going on with you" Delores said. Curtis looked away from his mother. "Mommy I love Marissa. I know she's no good for me and I know things will never be the same again." He said. "Curtis I'm not talking about Marissa and I'm not talking about the women you running with. What I'm talking about is why you're doing it and what you're running from. You're running from your past son, the abuse you suffered as a child. Honey what he did was bad but you have got to let go and forgive him and forgive yourself. You didn't do anything wrong you were only a child. How could you have helped yourself? You did what you had to do to survive" Tears were streaming down Delores's face. It hurt her to no end to see her child still suffering from the pain of the sexual abuse he suffered from his own father. It hurt her that she stayed with him so long even though she didn't know he was doing that to her son, she knew he was abusing him. She had long forgiven him and herself for the abuse now all she wanted was healing for her child. Curtis stood up and paced back and forward on the porch. "Sit down son" she grabbed his arm and he sat down.

"Honey look at me" Curtis continued to look at the ground. "Sweetheart I know you don't like to talk about this but you have to let it out. It's eating you alive and you don't even know it" Delores said. "What do you want me to say mama? What is it you want to hear from me?" Curtis said to his mother angrily. "Baby I want you to go and talk to somebody" "I already talked to somebody!" Curtis snapped at his mother. "That was for your anger problems honey. This person I want you to talk to is a specialist and she can help you if you will allow it. Please son for me?" Curtis looked at his mother and the tears running down her face. He hated to see his mother and sister cry. It hurt him so he gave in and said "Ok mama anything for you." Delores reached over and hugged him tightly and kissed him on his cheek. "Thank you, I love you Curtis Abney." Curtis hugged his mother tight and said "I love you to mama." Delores got up and went inside the house when she came back she had a card in her hand and handed it to Curtis. "Her name is Felicia May Stevenson and she specializes in sexual abuse counseling. She's the daughter of one of my friends here in the community and she's said to be very good at what she does. She's kind of pricey but that's not a problem for you." She handed him the card. Curtis took it and looked at it and put it in his pocket. "Promise me son you will make an appointment as soon as possible."

Curtis shook his head and said, "I will mama." He put the glass of half drank lemonade down and he kissed his mother on her cheek and said "I have to go mama I'll call you later" He said. "Make sure you call that woman and make an appointment, hear? If you don't I'll know." Delores said. Curtis smiled at his mother and said, "I know mama, I know." He walked off the porch and got back in his car. He waved to his mother and pulled away. Delores took a deep breath, she felt better. She felt like she really got through to him this time. She intended to check up on him to make sure he did what he said he was going to do.

As Curtis drove he thought about his mother's teary-eyed face and knew he couldn't let her down and maybe there was something to this Felicia chick. Maybe she could help him out. The truth is his mother was right he wasn't happy. In fact he was quite miserable. He knew he didn't really want a relationship with Strawberry or any of the other women he had slept with he didn't even want a relationship with Marissa. She was just what was familiar to him. Curtis vowed to give counseling a real shot this time. He pulled over and called the number on the card and made an appointment for the following week.

New York

Yvette, Krystal and Tonya walked tall and proud as they stepped in the lobby of the Plaza Hotel. The rooms at the Plaza started from $636 and up for the suites with king sized beds. Yvette always went for the best. When she booked their rooms she knew it was too pricey for their company so she booked it on her credit card with no problem. Tony paid all of her bills and he would pay this one with no questions asked. They walked up to the counter to check in. Tonya was so impressed she had never stayed in the Plaza Hotel before. Krystal was used to it but she didn't let on and of course Yvette was used to it because when she and Tony traveled it was first class all the way. They received their room cards and signed their papers and the bellhop escorted them to their rooms, which were all on the same floor right down the hall from one another. They got settled in, unpacked and agreed to meet in Yvette's room to have a bite to eat while they discussed the party they were hosting. They would go over any last minute details that needed to be addressed and make sure they had all their T's crossed and I" dotted.

They decided to meet in Yvette's room because she hadn't been feeling well on the plane. They wanted her to rest up for the big event. Yvette ordered lunch for them so it would be ready when they got to her room. Then she tried to get a quick nap before the girls showed up. Her back had been hurting so much lately and she was still having light cramps. She had no energy she was always tired. She'd been to the doctor and he told her to relax and try to stay off of her feet as much as possible but Yvette had been so busy with work and preparing for the New York trip that she had hardly gotten any rest. But she told herself after the event she would lay low for a while. She would take a week off of work and just relax with her feet up.

Yvette heard a knock at the door and she got up and walked over to the door. Instinct made her look through the peephole. It was room service bringing up their lunch. He rolled the cart over to the table and left it there. Yvette tipped him and he left. She called Krystal and Tonya to let them know that lunch was there. Ten minutes later Tonya was knocking on Yvette's door. Yvette got up and opened the door. "Hey girl, how you feeling?" Tonya asked. Yvette walked back to the chase lounge and sat down. "I am feeling better than I did on the plane" "Well put your feet up and let's eat girl. I am starving." Tonya said. Yvette put her legs up on the chase and lay back. Tonya rolled the cart closer to the table in the middle of them. She lifted the lids on the serving trays. "Mmm smells delicious." They had given Yvette their orders so each one of them had what they wanted. Tonya ordered a bacon cheeseburger with fries and a salad, Krystal ordered a steak sandwich with fries and a salad and Yvette was still queasy so she was eating light. She ordered a chicken sandwich with a side salad and ranch dressing.

Twenty minutes later Krystal showed up. Yvette and Tonya were almost done with their food when she sat down to join them. "Girl what took you so long?" Tonya asked. "I was on the phone with the guy from the venue there's a problem with our deposit. I know I made the deposit over the phone when I booked the place. I even have a confirmation number to prove it." Yvette and Tonya looked at each other with worried looks on their faces. Krystal held up her hand and said "Don't worry I gave him the confirmation number and he said he's going to look it up and call me back." "Well even if he can't find it you can have the credit card company confirm the payment right?" Tonya asked. "Yeah I supposed so but I hope he finds it otherwise I don't know what we are going to do with no place to have our event." Krystal said. "Well don't panic Krissy we'll get this all worked out. Eat your food" Yvette said to Krystal. "Let's go over everything else ok? Yvette said. They went over all the details even down to their wardrobe. When they had discussed everything Yvette could see that Krystal was still worried about the deposit. "Girl listen, if we have to move this event we just have to move it. Let's not start worrying about things we can't change." Krystal nodded indicating she understood but she was still concerned.

"Ok come on get up we are going out" Yvette said. "Yvette no, you need to lay down and get some rest girl I'll be fine once I hear back from them about this deposit." Tonya cleared away their lunch dishes and pushed the cart outside the door. Krystal's cell phone rang; it was the venue regarding their deposit. Krystal answered the phone it was a very short conversation. She closed her phone and looked at the girls and said "We have a problem. They have somehow misplaced our deposit and as of right now we have no place to have our event." Krystal put her two index fingers to either side of her head and massaged her temples. "Ok let's not panic. We have to think right now" Yvette said. "Did you tell them to call our credit card company?" "Yes I mentioned that earlier but he said that was not his responsibility" "Well why don't we just make another deposit?" Yvette said. "We can't afford to do that and who's to say they didn't get the deposit and just trying to hustle us?" "But this is supposed to be a replicable business do you really think they're hustling us?" Tonya asked. "I don't know. Why else could they not get our deposit?" "Have you called the credit card company maybe they didn't get it." Krystal shook her head. "Let's call the credit card company," Yvette said. "Well, wait a minute did you tell him we were going try and work this out so he wouldn't book anybody else in our spot?" "He said to call him back when I figure out what we're going to do" "That's good cus at least we have until tomorrow night to figure this out." Yvette said. Krystal picked up the phone and dialed the number on the back of the credit card. While she did that Yvette hooked up her laptop and she and Tonya went to work on finding another place to hold their event in case things didn't work out. Yvette thought about the place where Tony had his last fight and Googled it.

She remembered Tony saying he knew the owner Frank Marino. He used to be a part of his training crew but now he owned his own coliseum. She got the name and the number and called him up; she knew exactly what to say. "Hello may I speak with Frank Marino please? Yes, hi Frank you don't know me. I'm Yvette Williams, Tony Riche's fiancée. How are you? Good, listen I'm having a bit of a dilemma. You see I'm in the promoting business and I have a huge event tomorrow night maybe you've heard about it The Big Pay Back after party in light of the new movie that has just come out. Oh good you have heard about it, well look we were booked to have the event….that's right well the owner is claiming they misplaced our deposit and we know it was made. We've even tried to get them to call the credit card company to verify it but they won't hear of it. By us not being from New York we didn't know if he is trying to hustle us or what. But anyway we are just trying to line up another location in case this one doesn't work out for us. Do you think you would be able to help us out? Money would no problem as I said I'm Tony's fiancée. It's scheduled for tomorrow night; oh great are you sure? Do you need to call me back or check your books for tomorrow? Great! Well I'll keep you informed on what's going on but I most certainly appreciate this. Is it available for us to come and view? Great! No problem, give us about an hour maybe an hour and a half and we'll be right over. Ok thank you so much. I will and you take care ok. Bye." "Good news we may have a place if this one doesn't work for us. The coliseum it's owned by Frank Marino one of Tony's old trainers and he said we can come by and view the place if we want to. I told him to give us an hour or so. What do you think?" Tonya was nodding her head in agreement and Krystal was also but she was still on hold with the credit card company. "Yes, I see. Well is there something you can fax me some sort of confirmation? Very good here's the fax number." Krystal read off the fax number that was on the fax machine in the room then waited for the fax to come through.

Five minutes later the fax came through and Krystal disconnected the call. She picked up the fax and read it. It did show that their deposit was made. Krystal called the Venue back "Yes Jason, I just received a fax from my credit card company and it is showing that the deposit we made was received by your company. What do you mean you don't have it? Krystal was getting upset. "I have proof in my hand right now that your company received the deposit. Give me your fax number and I'll forward it to you right now. What do you mean it doesn't matter? So you're telling me even though I have proof that your company received my deposit my company still does not have a place to hold its event? If you knew you hadn't received our deposit why wouldn't you call us at least a week in advance to let us know? Why would you wait until the day before the event to inform us that you still don't have our deposit? You know what, there is no need for that sir you'll be hearing from our attorney good bye." And Krystal ended the call. "What did he say?" Yvette said. "He said there was no need to fax him the invoice from the credit card company because he still doesn't see our deposit on his books. He said it's going to take some time to sort this matter out and unless we make another deposit today we cannot use their facilities."

"Uh uh he cannot do this," Tonya said. "You know what it doesn't even matter cus after this I don't even want to deal with these people anymore? Let's just go and see Yvette's guy and see what his place looks like." "I agree" Yvette said. "Alright but what if we don't like this place? What if it's not big enough? What are we going to do then?" Tonya said. "We'll make this work y'all. Come on let's just go and see Frank and take it from there." Yvette said. They all took a cab to Frank's location. And when they got there they couldn't believe their eyes his place was huge and nice. They expected some little rinky dink place since he was an ex-trainer of Tony's they didn't think he made that much money but working for a world champ obviously paid well. They walked in and were further impressed. Everybody was very professional and was dressed in uniforms. Yvette asked the first person she saw where she could find Frank. They were immediately escorted to the office area of the coliseum where they met with Frank Marino. Frank was an Italian man with black curly hair.

He was very polite and very pleasant. He treated Yvette and the girls with the utmost respect. He gave them a good deal since he knew Tony and they were booked for tomorrow evening. Now all they had to do was start alerting the media that their event location had changed. That was going to take a little work but they were confident they could pull it off. When they returned to their hotel they were ecstatic. They headed right back to Yvette's room to start making the necessary calls to get their event location announced on all the radio stations and in the newspapers. They also had some emergency flyers printed up so they could have them passed out at all the clubs and movie theaters and just post them on the walls in the subways and stores. They had a lot of work to do so they got busy. Krystal started by contacting all of the radio stations she was already plugged in with to have them to announce the change of venue for their event. She had already purchased airtime for them to announce the event anyway so asking them to revise it was no problem. They were running the announcement during every commercial on two of the major stations.

Yvette got on the phone with the printing company who printed their flyers and asked them to do an emergency order that they could pick up the same day. She had them to print up at least 600 hundred of each so they could go around town and post them. Krystal called Jason back and let him know they would definitely be moving their event and to reemphasize that their attorney would be calling him. She also told him they would be posting a flyer outside the venue of their changed location. Then she put a call in to their attorney to get the legal ball rolling. She also faxed over their contract they had with Frank so that he could read over it and make sure everything was on the up and up. Tonya was busy calling all of the celebrity's managers to let them know what was going on. An hour and a half later they had all of the big details out of the way now all they needed to do is go and pick up the flyers and start handing them out all over town as much as they could since they only had six hundred. They took a cab to the printer's to pick up the order. They looked at them to make sure the location address was correct. Everything looked fine so they split them up and took separate cabs to different sides of town to hand out and post the flyers. Krystal made a quick stop at the New Yorker and other smaller papers to place their Ad.

By the time they all met back at the hotel it was almost 8:30 p.m. they were exhausted especially Yvette. They met back in her room and went over everything again to make sure there would be no more surprises for tomorrow. They knew the radio stations were on the ball because they had been listening while in the cabs to various stations the cabbies were playing. Krystal had already gotten the go ahead from their attorney everything was good with their contracts so they signed it and had the contract delivered back to Frank. When he received it he called them to say everything looked good. Finally they were done for the day. Krystal and Tonya were heading back to their rooms when Yvette called out "Hey y'all go ahead and grab your outfits for tomorrow. There over on the chase and the shoes are in the boxes on the floor with your names on them." They grabbed their outfits and shoes and said good night to Yvette and they were gone. Yvette headed straight to the bathroom and undressed and took a nice long bath. She sat in the bath water basking in the luxurious warmth and comfort of the water. She was also checking her text messages and answering emails. When she came to Tony's text it appeared he was furious with her. Yvette had not been answering her calls that were not related to the situation they were dealing with. She knew Tony had called her several times but she ignored the calls not wanting to interrupt the mission she was on. She was a little upset with him anyway because before she left for New York he was acting so nonchalant toward her. She felt like he was treating her kind of cold. The voice mails he had left her were even worse than his texts. Yvette took a deep breath and dialed his cell number and Tony answered his phone yelling and screaming at her.

"Why the hell haven't you been answering my damn calls Yvette? I've called your ass six times and you didn't answer one damn time. You didn't even answer my text." "Tony I was busy we had a situation we had to handle and I'm just now getting back to the hotel" Yvette said sounding exhausted. "I understand you have a business to run but you don't have time for me? Yo man? If it wasn't for me y'all wouldn't have half the contacts and clients' y'all got and you want to blow me off? Naw that shit ain't cool Yvette. What if I had an emergency? You don't know what could have been going on with me; you just gone ignore me like that? I know what your problem is. You call yourself all upset and hurt with yo emotional ass cus I had some business to take care of and couldn't cater to your spoiled ass like I usually do. But you need to get over that shit on the real cus when my lil man get here I'ma have even less time for yo ass believe that!" Tony yelled. Tears welled up in Yvette's eyes she tried not to let them fall because she didn't want to be crying on the phone. She didn't want him to know he had hurt her feelings. Tony had never spoken to her this way since they had been together. His words were hurtful to her and she couldn't hold back her emotions. She tried to get her voice together so he wouldn't know she was crying.

"Tony I'm sorry I called you as soon as I had a chance to. You're right I shouldn't have ignored your calls and baby I apologize." She said. Yvette's voice began to crack and she started crying again. "Stop crying that's all you do now is cry like a baby. I don't need no sensitive ass wife like you. You better man up if you want to be with Tony Riche." He said. Yvette was crying now openly. She was trying to get Tony to calm down and listen to her but he kept right on yelling at her and saying mean and hurtful things to her then he hung up on her. Yvette dialed his number back three times and each time he ignored her calls just as she had his. She felt bad she wished she had taken his calls. She wished she could go back and do it all over again. Yvette didn't want Tony mad at her especially with her all the way in New York and him back at home.

She was scared he was going to go out and cheat on her. Yvette kept trying to reach Tony but each time he ignored her calls. She lay in the bathtub and cried her eyes out. She felt the hunger pains and felt the slight thumps from the baby kicking in her womb. She held her stomach and cried even harder. Finally when she couldn't cry any more she got out of the tub and dried off and got dressed for bed. Yvette's back was hurting again and she was having that slight crampy feeling in her stomach. She hurried and called room service to order her some dinner. She was hungry but didn't have an appetite for anything. She ordered a chicken breast sandwich with fries and pink lemonade. Yvette knew it would probably go to waste but she had to make an effort to eat something for the baby's sake. She also knew if Tony thought she was not taken care of herself and jeopardizing his baby he would be even more furious with her.

When her food came she forced herself to eat half the sandwich and a few fries before she threw it all up. Yvette sat on the bathroom floor crying. She was feeling so anxious since Tony yelled at her and she was worried he was going to go and lay up with Eleshia or whomever he was seeing these days. She brushed her teeth and rinsed her mouth out with mouthwash and tried it again. This time she ate slower and took smaller bites so she could keep the food down. When she felt satisfied she put the plate down and wiped her mouth and lay down. She picked up her cell phone and looked at it wanting to call Tony just once more. She just needed to know everything was alright between them before she went to sleep. She dialed his number again and again he ignored her so she left him a voice mail this time. "Tony baby I'm so sorry. I realize I was wrong honey but really we did have an emergency that we had to handle immediately. See the guy who we were booked with tomorrow night bailed out on us telling us he didn't receive our deposit and that we couldn't hold our event there. So we had to find someplace else right away and get the media to announce the change in location. I'm so sorry I guess I wasn't thinking sweetheart. Please forgive me. Tony please I need to talk to you. I just need to hear your voice before I go to sleep." Yvette was crying as she talked in the phone. She ended the message and lay in the bed with tears slowly rolling down her face. Soon she fell asleep.

The next morning Yvette was awaken by her cell phone ringing in her ear. She had fallen asleep all night with it lying on her pillow. She jumped and quickly picked up the phone and answered it hoping it was Tony. It was Krystal "Hey sleepy head get up." Yvette's heart sank at the sound of Krystal's voice. "Good morning" Yvette said sounding disappointed. "Wow that sounded really sincere" Krystal said sarcastically. "I'm sorry girl I'm just tired is all. What time is it? "It is time to get your butt up we have work to do mama. We tried to let you sleep in a while but time is wasting mommy we gotta get in gear, now get up and get yourself together boo. I'll see you in about 30 minutes. Ok?" Krystal said. "Yeah ok." She said. Yvette closed her phone and sat up in the bed rubbing her eyes. She was hoping Tony was calling her back to apologize. She reluctantly got up and walked into the bathroom and started the shower. She walked over to the sink and picked up her toothbrush and started to brush her teeth. She looked at herself in the mirror hating her reflection. Yvette was so mad at herself for not answering Tony's call yesterday. If she had just answered he wouldn't be mad at her and wouldn't possibly be lying up with another woman right now. "I don't want to assume the worst." Yvette thought to herself, it's just that her history with Tony taught her to always be suspicious of him when it came to other women. She wanted to trust him but the truth is she didn't anymore. There was a time when she believed he loved her and only her and would do anything in the world for her. But now, well it seemed like he had grown tired of her. Yvette spit and rinsed her mouth. She put her toothbrush away and removed her clothes and got in the shower.

By noon she was dressed and they were heading over to Frank's place to make sure all the equipment had arrived and that everything was where it needed to be. When they got there the equipment had been set up and some of the musicians had already arrived for sound check. They inspected the dressing rooms making sure each celebrity had what they requested in their rooms. Frank's place was really nice and clean they were really impressed with how he ran his establishment.

Once they were satisfied with everything at the Coliseum they moved on to the radio station. Krystal had arranged for them to go on live on the air to discuss the event and to announce, once again that the location had been changed. So they headed to the radio station. From there they had another interview lined up on the local news station to promote the event again. Krystal had pulled out all the stops. She used her radio connects to hook up the last minute interviews which worked out well for them; it gave them more exposure and if they were able to pull of the night's event after the last minute change in location, it would put them on the map. Basically the whole city would see that Diva Promotions knows how to throw a party and how to overcome the last minute emergencies. After their interviews and checking on a few more last minute details they headed back to the hotel to have a late lunch and rest up before their next appointment. Yvette had arranged for them to be at Elizabeth Arden at 5p.m. to get the full spa treatment including makeup and hair. They ate in their own rooms this time.

Yvette lay in the bed with her plate resting on her lap flipping through channels on the television. She had already called Tony several times but he was still ignoring her calls. She was so upset she wanted to cry again but she refused to. Her pregnancy had made her so sensitive she cried at the drop of a hat. Yvette had eaten half of her steak and a small portion of her baked potato before she dozed off to sleep. She had been sleeping about an hour when her cell phone rang but she was so tired she slept right through it. When she did wake up it was time to get ready to go to Elizabeth Arden. She met the girls in the lobby at 4:30 p.m. when she checked her massages she was disappointed that she had missed Tony's call again. Yvette called him three times but he didn't answer. She left him a voice mail "Honey please call me back. I was taking a nap when you called. I wanna talk to you sweetie please call me." Krystal and Tonya looked at each other with a frown on their faces wondering why she was begging Tony to call her. Krystal knew something must have happened that she hadn't mention to them but she didn't pry. She wondered about Yvette though. She didn't believe Tony was the man for her best friend. She prayed for the day when Yvette would wake up and realize it too.

When they walked into The Red Door of Elizabeth Arden and entered the lobby it was absolutely beautiful and fancy. They were immediately taken into the back to change out of their clothes for massages. After massages came the facials then nails and hair and makeup would be last. As they lay on the massage tables waiting for their masseuse to arrive Tonya said to Yvette "So girl what was all that begging you was doing earlier? Yvette looked up at Tonya a little offended by her lack of tact so she responded "None of your business." Tonya looked up at Yvette with a frown on her face. "Dag you ain't got to be nasty about it sweetie; I was just asking a question." She said. "And I was just answering a question." Yvette responded "Yvette, sweetie why are you getting so defensive? I'm not trying to pry in your business if you rather not talk about just say I don't want to talk about it." Tonya said. Krystal was looking over at Yvette from the table she was lying on; she said to Yvette "Honey did something happen?" Yvette with her head still faced down on the table rolled her eyes before she spoke "Nothing happened I just missed his calls since I've been here and I really wanted to talk to him that's all." Krystal nodded her head "Ok, I understand why you would be anxious to talk to him."

Tonya looked over at Yvette and rolled her eyes. She knew that was not the truth and so did Krystal. They both knew Yvette well just as she knew them well and they all knew when something was bothering the other that's how close they were. Just then their masseuses entered the room; the conversation was ended. Yvette was a bit tensed when the masseuse started but she began to relax and loosen up as she went to work on her muscles. There was soft relaxing music playing in the background it was so luxurious. She couldn't help but close her eyes and allow herself to be taken away by the calming effect of the masseuse's hands and the lolling sounds of the music. The massage lasted an hour but Yvette wanted it to last longer but they were pressed for time. She reluctantly sat up when the masseuse was done. They were shown to the sauna area where they were able to lay out for twenty minutes in the steamy rock filled room. It was so nice it made you feel like you were in a garden with all kinds of flowers and greens and warm rocks to lie on. There was little talking between them not because they were mad at one another but because they were enjoying the treatment. Yvette was surprised that she didn't allow her mind to think on Tony not one time. After the sauna they were shown to the showers.

They were given luxurious soaps and towels as they entered the beautiful spacious shower area. Everything was immaculate and shining. The girls looked around before they got in the showers. "Wow this place is awesome." Krystal said. "It's so clean." "Well it should be for how much they charge." Yvette responded. There were several personal showers and one community shower that would fit at least seven women. The girls chose the personal showers. "This was a good idea Yvette." Tonya said out loud over the shower. "Yes it was girl. We needed this." Krystal said. "Thank you." Yvette said. After their showers they were shown to the salon area where they all got their hair shampooed and conditioned then their facials were applied. They sat back comfortable in the salon chairs as the facial formula dried on their face. "I read somewhere this place is world renown. Women pay a lot of money to come here for their facials." Krystal said. "As hard as my face feels right now I hope so and did it happen to mention if it was any good for us sistas? Tonya said. Yvette and Krystal laughed. "It's made for all women." A soft voice responded that didn't belong to Krystal or Yvette; it was one of the young women who had washed and shampooed their hair and applied their facials.

They all opened their eyes at the sound of the unfamiliar voice. "Well that's good to know." Tonya responded to the young woman before she left the room. They all looked at each other and laughed. "You got to watch what you say around here. I see the walls have ears." Tonya whispered as they all laughed. Yvette looked over at Tonya and said "T, I'm sorry for what I said earlier. Girl you know I didn't mean it and you know I love you." "Oh sweetie, don't sweat that. I know when something is bothering you. You my girl and all I was trying to do is help out." Tonya responded. "I know I'm just so stressed out that's all. Things have not been going well with Tony and I and I was just taking out my frustrations on you." "What's going on?" Krystal asked. Yvette shook her head "He's just been acting so distant lately and last night he basically told me off because I didn't answer his calls the day we got here. I tried to explain we were busy but he didn't want to hear it. And he called me again last night and I missed his call. When I called him back he didn't answer. I'm just a little stressed that's all." "Well look that's why we're here to chill out and relax so let's do that." Tonya said. Yvette nodded her head and closed her eyes again. Tonya looked over at Krystal as they both shook their heads and then closed their eyes. When their facials were all peeled away and their skin had been moisturized three beauticians were brought in to do their hair. By request they had three black beauticians to do their hair.

When they walked out of Elizabeth Arden two hours later they left looking like a million bucks. They left with a bag full of Elizabeth Arden makeup for touch ups when they needed it later. The bags were a gift for purchasing the all-inclusive package. With their hair, makeup and nails all done that left them an hour to go and get dressed back at the hotel and head over to the Coliseum. Yvette chose white and gold for them to wear. White was kind of their signature color. Yvette's dress was a slim fitting shell dress with one wide strap on the left shoulder and right side cut out to the hip with gold trimming and three gold chains across the cut out and a split in the front of the dress up to the upper part of her knee and she wore gold studded shoes. She wore it well and since she was only four months pregnant she still was not showing yet.

She chose for Krystal a white dress trimmed in gold. The back was out except for two gold crisscross straps in the back that reached around to the front of her dress. It looked almost like it was a two-piece because the gold trimming crisscrossed in front of the dress just below the breast area, which left the sides open. It also had a small train in the back. And Tonya's dress was similar to Yvette's because it was a one wide strap shoulder dress with the middle cut out in front and back trimmed in gold with one thin gold piece connecting both the top and the bottom of the dress together. Her dress had a small train in the back like Krystal's. They were all wearing similar shoes and looked stunning. Jovani made all the outfits and the shoes were Prada. Yvette hired a white limo for the evening and as the car pulled up to the Coliseum they stepped out looking like stars. There was a crowed already formed at the door. The security was tight and had the crowd well under control. As they walked to the door one security guard opened it for them. They got a few yells and screams from the crowd. Some of them recognized the Divas. They hurried back stage to make sure their celebrities were taken care of. They were relieved to find that Frank had taken very good care of their guests and everyone was satisfied. They headed over to the DJ booth to say hello to the one and only Kid Rock. They all knew him well from the radio industry so they kicked it with him for a while then moved on to Frank's office to take care of the final payment for the evening.

They were shown into his office. "Ladies you all look beautiful tonight. Please sit down. I have to tell you ladies I'm impressed with what you have been able to do in such a short amount of time. I think you are going to be very successful in this business. People like to do business with promoters who know what they're doing and who knows how to handle emergency situations with ease and finesse. I can tell you this much you made a name for yourself here in New York. I'll personally recommend your services." The girls looked at each other and smiled. "Thank You so much Frank. I can't tell you what a pleasure it's been working with you." Krystal said. "Yes you've been very professional and you have a nice place. I appreciate everything you've done." Yvette said. "Thank you for having our back at the last minute man. You're awesome and we would love to do business with you again soon." Tonya added. "Hey no problem I suspect we'll do more business together in the future. It looks like the house will be packed tonight and that's a good thing." Krystal handed Frank the envelope containing their final payment and concluded their business with him. By this time it was time for the doors to be opened. They stood in the DJ booth talking and laughing and toasting their success with the DJ Kid Rock. Yvette was having orange juice and Krystal and Tonya were having champagne. They watched the crowd come in. Soon it was time for them to take the stage so they left their glasses and was shown downstairs to the stage entrance. When they were introduced they heard the crowd go wild as they took the stage and did their thing. Tonya was always the more louder and vocal one of them. Yvette took it where she left off and Krystal was in between. All in all they were a great trio and the crowd loved them.

While the celebrities performed the girls went back stage to take photos with their guests before and after they performed. Then they took their promo shots and after all the celebrities performed they headed to the DJ booth to play with the crowd. The DJ area was no booth really it was more like a balcony that allowed the whole party to see the DJ and the DJ to see them. The crowd was hyped and the music was bumping. Yvette and Tonya did their thing with the crowd and then it was time to mingle amongst everybody. As they weaved through the crowd they were constantly stopped to sign an autograph or to take photos with other celebrities. As the evening wore down Yvette found a table to sit down and rest her feet and her back. She looked around at the crowd thinking, we really pulled it off tonight. I'm so proud of us. I wish I wasn't pregnant right now though as much as I want this baby I want to continue with my business as well and a baby will definitely slow me down. She thought to herself. But my child is my child and I'll find a way to make this work even if I have to hire a nanny. Krystal came and joined Yvette at the table. "Whew" she sat down fanning herself. "Girl you alright?" She asked. Yvette nodded her head. "Yeah I'm just resting my feet." Krystal looked at Yvette and said. "Yvette why don't you go ahead and head home tomorrow. Tonya and me will handle the last interviews we have lined up tomorrow. You've been really busy preparing for this trip and you did a great job with our outfits and your end of your responsibilities but you're pregnant and you do need your rest. Just go home and put your feet up and take a load off."

Yvette looked at Krystal offended. "You think I can't handle this?" She said. "Oh God no, honey that's not what I meant. I can see you're tired and you said your back was hurting earlier. You're in the early stages of your pregnancy and I don't want to see anything happen to you or the baby that's all." Krystal said. Yvette took a deep breath and exhaled and said, "I'm sorry. It's just that I was just sitting here thinking how I wished I wasn't pregnant right now with our business being so new and all. I love doing what we do and a baby will slow me down but I'll make it work." Krystal reached over and held Yvette's hand and said, "We'll make it work. I wouldn't dream of getting rid of you. The Divas Promotions would be no good without each other." Krystal said. Yvette laughed "I would like to just go home and rest and to talk to Tony since he thinks I'm avoiding him." She said. "There you go, so go ahead tomorrow take an early flight and we'll be along later." Yvette nodded in agreement. She was actually relieved because she did want to go home but not to rest but to see Tony and make sure everything was ok between them.

At 8 a.m. Yvette was on a first class flight back to Atlanta. She tried to call Tony again but his phone went straight to voicemail, which meant he had turned it off. She rested her head against the seat and closed her eyes. She had a two-hour flight so she decided to get some sleep. She awoke when she heard the captain announce they were coming into Hartsfield airport in Atlanta. Yvette stretched and yawned. She opened her purse and pulled out her mirror to check her face. She put on some lip-gloss and powdered her face then put her mirror away and waited for the plane to land. Ten minutes later they were landing. Yvette was so happy to be going home. All she wanted to do is to make up with Tony. She tried his cell phone again but still he had it turned off. Yvette went through baggage claim and gathered her bags then she put them on a cart and walked out to the curb to hail a cab. Thirty minutes later the cab pulled up in front of her house. Yvette paid the cabbie and got out the car. She walked up to the door with the cabbie following her with her bags. She got her key out and opened the door and went inside. She stood at the door until the cabbie had sat all of her bags inside the door. Yvette closed the door and walked down the steps.

Before she made it to the stairway Rosie appeared "Oh good morning ma'am, I didn't expect you until tomorrow." "Good morning Rosie. I came home early I wasn't feeling well." She said. As Yvette walked up the steps Rosie kept watching her which was odd. Yvette stopped and said "Is there something wrong Rosie?" Rosie looked kind of unsure or nervous maybe. "Oh no ma'am, everything is fine." She said. Yvette nodded and kept walking up the steps. Rosie watched her until she disappeared around the corner. She wrung her heads thinking "Oh my God. I feel so sorry for her." As Yvette reached the bedroom door she put her hand on the knob and walked in. The sight before her was unbelievable. Tony was in the bed making love to some woman who was screaming his name. It was the same woman she had heard over the phone when he was in Italy. They didn't know she was there because the woman was moaning and screaming. Yvette couldn't believe this. She held her hand to her heart. Her bottom lip was trembling as she fought the urge to cry. She started to run out but curiosity got the better of her and she wanted to see the woman's face. She walked slowly up to the bed and then to the side of it until she was able to see the woman he was in bed with. As she looked at the woman tears streamed down her face. It was her Eleshia, the woman she knew he loved or at least had feelings for. Yvette started to sob out loud. Tony jumped when he heard her. He jumped off of Eleshia immediately when he noticed she was standing there watching them. Eleshia sat up with the covers pulled to her chest in shock.

Yvette was hyperventilating she couldn't catch her breath. She started to move toward the door. Tony was already putting on his pants and yelling "Baby" He started to come for her but she turned and ran out of the door. Tony reached for her but he missed her as she ran passed him. He took off down the hall after her yelling "Baby, Baby come back." Yvette kept running as she reached the steps she was trying to take them two at a time so Tony couldn't catch her. Tony leaped for Yvette yelling, "Baby stop, stop running like that." Yvette didn't even look back she just wanted to get out of the house. She made it down four of the long steps before her foot twisted in the heel she was wearing and she went tumbling down the steps. She tried to stop herself but her foot had gotten caught in the dress she was wearing. Tony yelled when he saw her ankle twist and she went tumbling down the stairs. "Yvette! Baby" Tony ran down the stairs two at a time to reach Yvette lying at the bottom of the steps crying and screaming as she held her stomach. Rosie had come running out of the kitchen at the sound of Yvette's and Tony's screams. Tony reached Yvette and picked her up and carried her to the couch. "Baby I'm sorry." Yvette was screaming as she held her stomach. She felt overwhelming cramps like she had never experienced before. "Yvette what's wrong baby?" Yvette continued to scream. Tony jumped up and grabbed the phone and called 911. Eleshia watched from the top of the stairs wrapped up in a sheet. Tony was trying to calm Yvette down. He looked up and saw Eleshia standing there. He looked away and focused all of his attention on Yvette. Eleshia turned and walked away feeling jilted. She went back to the room and got dressed.

She came walking down the stairs in a huff as if she had something to be upset about. She walked up to the couch where Tony was holding Yvette and rocking her. Yvette was still crying and screaming ever so often when she felt a cramp. As Eleshia walked up to the couch she expected Tony to say something to her; to acknowledge her but he held on to Yvette even tighter and kept rocking her. Yvette looked Eleshia in the eyes as she stood over them. That woman stared back at Yvette with such hatred in her eyes. The same look Eva had in her eyes when she looked at Yvette. "This bitch got some nerve after she was just fucking my man. She got the nerve to look at me that way." Finally she walked out the front door and before she could slam it the paramedics were walking in. Tony got up when he saw the paramedics. He ran upstairs to finish getting dressed and grabbed his wallet. He rushed back downstairs as the paramedics was putting Yvette on the stretcher and taking her out the front door. Tony ran out behind them and ran right past Eleshia who was standing there watching. He jumped in the ambulance with Yvette before they shut the door. As the ambulance rolled away Eleshia watched with tears running down her face thinking "Eva was wrong he doesn't love me he loves her." Eleshia walked away.

Inside the ambulance Yvette held her stomach as tears were steady running down her face. She thought back to the conversation she had with Krystal about wishing she wasn't pregnant. All she wanted was to save her baby at this point nothing else mattered to her, not Tony and definitely not Eleshia. Yvette was so scared she kept holding her stomach as if she could keep her baby safe that way. She glanced at Tony and all she saw was sorrow on his face. Well she didn't care what he was feeling. If it weren't for him and that hoe she wouldn't be in danger of losing her baby right now. So screw Tony and his feelings she told herself. She glanced at him again and he was looking at her and he mouthed silently I'M SORRY. Yvette closed her eyes because she didn't care how sorry he was, the only thing that was important was the precious life on the inside of her. All she wanted to do was protect it from harm and danger and to bring it into this world safe and sound. Suddenly her broken heart no longer mattered to her. What Tony did to her didn't bother her at the moment. She began calling on God to save her baby.

God please save my child. Please don't let my baby die. Lord if you give this child a chance I swear I won't ask you for another favor again. Help me Lord please. My baby didn't do anything wrong. I'm sorry for what I said yesterday. I'm so sorry. I want my baby. I love my baby. Please God help me!!

The ambulance pulled up in front of the emergency room and Yvette was rushed in and pushed straight to the back. The doctors went to work on her. Her dress was cut to remove it from her body quickly her panties along with it. Yvette screamed as cramps and spasms over took her. She was balled up in the fetus position crying when all of a sudden she felt wet and cold. Yvette felt a pinch in her left arm and that was the last thing she remembered.

When Yvette opened her eyes she was lying in a hospital bed and Tony was sitting next to the bed with his head in his hands. She looked around the room and saw that it was a hospital suite. Her bed was the only bed in the room. She felt drowsy as she tried to focus her eyes. Her arm felt tight she moved her left arm and Tony lifted his head. His eyes were swollen and red when he looked at her. Yvette stared at him for a while trying to remember what happened and how she ended up in the hospital. It all came back to her in a rush. Her eyes widen as she remembered her baby. Yvette put her hand on her stomach and said "My baby" "Is my baby ok? She asked Tony. Tony looked at Yvette and said "They couldn't save the baby." Yvette began to cry and scream. Tony tried to calm her down but she was beyond controlling. He just wrapped his arms around her and hugged her and she hugged him back as she cried and screamed mourning the loss of her baby. The nurses came running into the room. Tony held up his hand to keep them from coming any closer. He wanted to hold her until she calmed down. They stood back and allowed them to have their personal time. When Yvette was done crying her throat hurt from all of the screaming she had done. But she felt so empty inside, like the life that was inside of her left with the baby. Her heart ached at the thought of her baby dying and never having a chance at life. Tony let Yvette go and the nurses came forward to take her vital signs. Yvette lay there feeling limp like a rag doll. All of her energy was gone. She stared straight ahead at nothing. Tony watched her with concern on his face. He had cried his eyes out when the doctors told him Yvette had lost the baby. He felt like it was his fault. If she had never walked in on him making love to Eleshia she would never had to run away and fallen down the stairs. He wouldn't blame her for hating him because right now he hated himself. Now to see how it was affecting Yvette made him feel even worse.

Now he had to call her mother and sisters and tell them what happened. And Krystal and Tonya and they were a force to be reckoned with. Tony felt like he needed some support of his own so he left the room while the nurse was still checking Yvette. As he was leaving the doctor had just arrived. He stepped outside the room to call his mother and brother and let them know what happened. He dialed Eva's number and she answered right away. "Hello my son, how are you? Tony paused for a moment to hold back the tears. "Mama she lost the baby." Tony said. "I'm sorry son to hear that but Eleshia called me and told me everything." "She called you? "Yes and she told me what happened. Eleshia said Yvette walked in on you and her and she got upset and ran out and fell down the stairs." Tony couldn't hold back the tears any longer. "Mama it was all my fault. If she hadn't walked in on us she would still be pregnant." He cried into the phone. "Stop all that crying boy. Listen it is not your fault dear heart. She was the one who put her own self in danger by running down a flight of stairs. What pregnant woman runs down a flight of stairs? "But she was upset mama. She was hurt and it is my fault." He said.

"You listen to me now boy. You didn't do anything wrong. You've been promised to Eleshia from day one and you are not married yet so you were not wrong. Those American women don't take good care of themselves. If she were strong like an island woman she wouldn't have killed the baby. That's what you need son a good sturdy woman who can take a little fall and still hold on to the baby she carries in her womb. She is no good for you son. And stop blaming yourself it is her fault. She was always throwing up and lying down sick all the time. An island woman can take morning sickness and still work around the house and never allow it to bother her. American women are pampered and spoiled and they have no idea what it takes to please a man or keep a man. They're weak and fragile; they're no better than little children. Stop beating yourself up and look at the one who's really to blame her not you son." Tony listened to his mother. Although he didn't think it was Yvette's fault for losing the baby but he did think she was a bit spoiled and milked the pregnancy. She couldn't take having sex with him without crying. He always felt like he was hurting her. Tony said goodbye to his mother and went back into the room to sit with Yvette. After talking to his mother he sat there next to Yvette staring at the television but not watching it. Tony glanced at Yvette he didn't want to believe what his mother had said about her.

He knew himself that it wasn't her fault. He regretted what he had to do next which is calling her family and let them know what happened. He spoke to Yvette. "What did the doctor say?" Yvette looked Tony in the eyes for a second then she turned her head as if he hadn't spoken to her. "Yvette what did the doctor say?" This time she didn't look at him and still she didn't answer him. Tony gave up and left the room. He walked to the nurses' station and asked "Is Yvette's Williams doctor available?" Her nurse stood up and said "I'm her nurse what can I help you with?" He walked over to where she sat behind the desk and said "I wasn't in the room when the doctor came in and I was wondering what he had to say about her condition? "Well as you know the doctor had to perform a dilation and curettage also known as a D&C, which means he had to perform a surgical procedure to remove the contents of the uterus. She may experience some abdominal pains and her stomach will be sore for a few days. That's due to the vacuum aspiration he used to remove the fetus from the uterine walls. Much like the procedure performed in an abortion. She'll be bleeding for probably five days to week that's common. He does want to keep her overnight just to keep an eye on her. I don't know if you know that she was four months pregnant which is why the doctor felt the D&C was necessary. But the doctor is very optimistic that she'll be able to conceive again as soon as her body recovers.

Now I would like to prepare you for the emotional distress that is taking place in her now. She's probably feeling guilty or in denial and maybe even numb. These are all natural feelings after a miscarriage. She'll get over it but be patient with her. She may experience fatigue, trouble sleeping, difficulty concentrating, and loss of appetite and frequent episodes of crying. The hormonal changes that occur after a miscarriage may intensify these symptoms. The important thing to remember is, this is all natural feelings for women after such a loss. What she needs right now is rest and time to grieve. Do you have any questions?" Tony had listened to the nurse and understood what she was saying. "No not at this time." "Ok if you need anything I'll be out here or you can just press the nurse's button on the remote alright?" "Alright and thank you." He said. "You're very welcome."

Tony walked away and went back into Yvette's room. She had the covers over her head. Tony walked up to her and tried to pull the covers back but she had a firm hold on them and wouldn't let go. "Yvette what's wrong baby? He continued to pull and she tightened her grip on the covers. Tony gave up he walked out of the room. He tried not to be too concerned about her mood. Just like the nurse had said, "Let her grieve." Tony decided now was a good time to call her family and let them know what happened. He dialed her mother's number and she answered. He proceeded to tell her that Yvette had lost the baby and she was in the hospital. He also told her he would fly her and the rest of the family down if they wanted to be with Yvette. He felt so guilty. He didn't tell Yvette's mother how she loss the baby although she kept asking he didn't divulge that information. Of course Ernestine wanted to come down to be with her baby in her time of bereavement. Tony made the arrangements for her to fly out the following day so she would be there when Yvette got out of the hospital.

Then he called Krystal but she didn't answer her phone so he left a message for her to call him. He didn't want to leave that type of message on her voicemail. He decided to try Tonya but she didn't answer her phone either so he left her the same message. He went back into the room with Yvette and sat next to her in the chair by her bed. When he came back into the room she still had the covers over her head. He looked at her for a while but he didn't bother to remove the covers. He sat and watched television until he fell asleep. Yvette had fallen asleep herself under the covers but now she was awake. She removed the covers from her head and turned and looked at Tony. She watched him sleep for a while thinking. "I hate him. Look at him just sitting there like he cares about me. I lost my child because of him and I'll never forgive him for that. I've forgiven many things but this is unforgiveable as far as I'm concerned. If I had just stayed in New York I would still have my baby. I would still be pregnant."

Tears poured from Yvette's eyes. "I was in such a rush to get home to him and for what to watch him having sex with another woman. I should have been more concerned about my baby and me, not him. I want my baby back. I wanna feel the little thumps I use to feel. I wanna feel queasy and sick." Yvette started to shake her head and started to sob out loud. Her crying woke Tony up. He jumped up and sat on the bed next to her and held her as she cried. Yvette jerked him off of her. She didn't want to be touched by him. She didn't even want him sitting next to her. When she pulled away from him he sat back and just stared at her. He was in pain too and all he wanted to do was hold her until the pain subsided for both of them. "Yvette baby I'm so sorry. I never meant to hurt you and I never wanted anything to happen to our baby. Please forgive me. I love you." Yvette was crying and rocking and holding herself. She didn't believe for one second that he loved her. She thought back to all the abuse she'd taken from Leonard and the heartache of his cheating and Tony's cheating. How much can a woman take? She wondered why the men in her life hurt her so. What was it about her that was so unlovable? Tony sat back down and dropped his head in his hands and wept silently.

When Yvette had recovered from crying she lay there silent just staring into space thinking. Since she had found out she'd lost the baby she hadn't talked to God. She kept thinking she should but she just didn't have the words to say. Tony noticed she had stopped crying and he said to her in an attempt to cheer her up "I called your mother and told her what happened and she's coming in tomorrow to be with you." Yvette stopped rocking she was thinking to herself, no this Negro didn't go and tell my mama what happened. I wonder just how much he told her. I don't need her in my ear telling me to hold on to a good man. Lord help me. Tony was hoping to get a response out of Yvette but she still said nothing to him. Tony just shook his head and made one last attempt to talk to her.

"Baby please, talk to me. I know you're hurting and I'm hurting too. I promise you I'm sorry. I don't know what else to say to you baby. I know what I did was wrong but I loss something too. I wanted our baby just as much as you did. But the doctor said we could try again. I promise I'll take you somewhere anywhere. You can relax and put this all behind you. And when we get married you don't have to work you can stay home and just raise our kids. It'll be different Yvette I swear. Just tell me you forgive me and talk to me. I wanna be here for you boo." Yvette heard every word he said but still she didn't have anything to say to him. What she was feeling had nothing to do with walking in and catching him on top of another woman. She felt numb inside. She wanted to feel something but right now she felt nothing not even sympathy for Tony and his bereavement.

Now common sense told her he must be hurting too. But the numbness she was experiencing didn't allow for any sympathy or empathy for him. When she was napping she had a dream she was holding her baby boy in her arms and he was absolutely beautiful. He had Tony's complexion and had his pretty curly black hair and he even had blue eyes. He was perfect. Then all of a sudden the blanket that he was wrapped in crumbled in her arms because the baby was no longer in it. She felt such overwhelming sadness even while she had slept. Tony's cell phone was ringing. He picked it up looked at the caller ID and saw that it was Krystal calling him back. He stepped out of the room and took the call. "Hello" Tony said. "Hi Tony its Krystal, I got your message what's up?" Krystal and Tonya were on the airplane on their way back to Atlanta. "I was calling you to let you know that Yvette loss the baby." Krystal's heart sank at those words. She clutched her hand to her chest and said "What?" "Yeah it happened as soon as she got home. She fell down the stairs and had to be rushed to the hospital." "Oh my God" Tonya looked at Krystal alarmed. "I just wanted you to know." "Oh my God. How is she

PURPOSE IN THE PAIN

doing?" "Not good, she's crying off and on and she won't even talk to me." "Tony I'm so sorry to hear about this. How are you doing?" "I'm hurt and just trying to stay strong for Yvette. But I'm ok right now." He said. "We're on the plane now heading back to Atlanta please let Yvette know how sorry I am and as soon as this plane land we'll be heading straight to the hospital." Tony told Krystal what hospital and room they were in and they ended the call. Tonya was looking at Krystal with concern on her face. "What happened? What's wrong with Yvette?" Tears were falling down Krystal's face as she felt sorrow for her friend. "Tony said she loss the baby." "What? How did that happen? "He said it happened as soon as she got home. He said she fell down the stairs and had to be rushed to the hospital." Tonya clutched her hand to her chest. "Oh no, poor Yvette how's she doing?" Tonya asked. "He said she wasn't doing too well." "As soon as this plane lands we need to head right to the hospital." Tonya said. "I know that's what I told Tony." They both sat there in silence thinking about their friend as the plane headed toward Atlanta.

Yvette lay in the hospital bed looking at the ceiling and thinking. It was close to 7:30 p.m. and Tony had left to go home and take a shower and change his clothes. He had promised Yvette he would be back. The truth is he didn't want to be around when Krystal and Tonya showed up and Yvette told them the real reason she fell down the steps and lost the baby. Yvette turned her head when she noticed something bright red out of the corner of her eye on her left hand side towards the door. Somebody was outside her door with a beautiful bouquet of red roses. She strained her neck to see who was holding them. Krystal peeked around the corner smiling as she and Tonya walked in with red roses and balloons. "Hey how are you?" Krystal said as she walked forward with the roses. She hugged and kissed Yvette and Tonya did the same. They both sat on either side the bed and they lay with her rocking her as she started to cry again. She was glad to see somebody who really cared for her. "It's alright sweetie. You cry, let it out." Krystal said to Yvette. "We love you boo and we're so sorry." Yvette allowed her friends to comfort her. When she was done crying and felt calmer they let her go and sat up still sitting on either side of her. Yvette adjusted the bed so she would be sitting up. "How you feeling baby?" Tonya asked. "I'm feeling a little sore." Yvette held her stomach. "Other than that how do you feel?"

She asked. "I feel numb right now. I've had a few dreams about holding my baby and then having him just disappear in my arms. That was the worst one. I felt like I came so close to having him in my life then all of a sudden he's gone; not there anymore. I feel empty inside. I wanna feel him move on the inside of me. I wanna feel those little thumps I use to feel." Yvette was crying again. Tonya handed her a tissue to wipe her eyes. "Sweetie what did the doctor say?" Krystal asked. "He said I would be able to have kids again. He suggested I wait until my body heals to try again." "That's a good thing boo." Tonya said. Yvette nodded her head because she believed it was a good thing. "How did you fall down the steps? Krystal asked. Yvette took a deep breath and related how she came to fall down the steps. When she had finished telling the story Krystal and Tonya was seeing red because they were so mad at Tony.

"That dirty bastard" Tonya said. "When I asked him how you fell down the stairs he totally avoided that question" Krystal said. "Where's he now?" Tonya asked. "He said he was going home to take a shower and change his clothes." "Did he even call your family? "Yeah he called my mother. She'll be here tomorrow afternoon." Yvette said. "Yvette I've tried to stay out of your business in the past but this is too much and as your friend I feel I have to say something. Honey you deserve better. It's one thing to have him cheating on you and you can't see it but when he brings it home and you walk in and catch him; honey he don't care anything about your feelings nor does he have any respect for you. Now is the time to walk away from this mess. I know you love him but what does love have to do with it? This is about you and your feelings and respect for yourself. At some point you have to put an end to this foolishness in your life. I know you may not be ready to hear this right now but it is what it is. Take it for what it is and move on. God has your back and he always has. You found the strength to leave an abusive marriage you can find the strength to walk away from this. It's not healthy for you and it wouldn't have been healthy for your baby. God knew that and maybe that's why this had to happen, baby, so that God could get you to open your eyes and really look at your surroundings. You've fooled yourself long enough sweetie it's time to let it go." Yvette listened to Krystal without any tears over the words she'd spoken. What she had just said was confirmation to what God had been telling her. This was a huge wakeup call from the Lord and now was the time to heed to it. "You're right Krystal. I've known this for a long time but I tried to ignore it but it's the truth. It is what it is. There's no other way to look at it or sugar coat it. I haven't thought much about what I was gone do tomorrow when I left this hospital but I don't think I can go back there anyway. I can't lie in that same bed that he was in with another woman." She said. "You'll come and stay with me." Krystal said. "Or me" Tonya said. Yvette nodded her head in agreement. "It's gonna be alright boo. We're here for you" Tonya said. "We'll be how we use to be. Hitting the jazz clubs and bars and just hanging out spending girl time with each other. We'll be able to focus on the business more. I think we about to blow up boo. This New York trip put us out there" Tonya said. "You'll come and stay with me Tonya only has a one room condo." Krystal said. "Yes I do but the room is yours if you want it baby" Tonya said. Yvette smiled and hugged them both. "What would I do without friends like y'all? Y'all have been a blessing in my life. I love you both" Yvette said. They sat with her and talked about the last interview they had in New York with the early morning show. Yvette laughed at the stories they told her about being on the set and back stage. She was able to forget for a moment about her pain. Though she still felt hollow inside she did laugh.

ABOUT THE AUTHOR

Angela was born in Chicago and raised in the south suburbs of Beacon Hill, IL. She is divorced and is a mother of two, daughter Amber and son Lamont Jr. She's also a woman of faith, an author and a playwright. She began her writing in 2008 when she started writing poems, songs and blogs. She wrote her first blog for her therapist and named it "A Day in the Life of an Addict" The blog outlined Angela's 19 year battle with bulimia. It was then that her therapist told her she was a phenomenal writer and encouraged her to keep writing. In 2009 things in her marriage took a terrible turn for the worst and she had to take a leave of absence from work. It was then that God gave her the vision to write "The Power of Love" She wrote every day until in 2010 her life was turned upside down and she was forced to separate from her husband. With nothing but the clothes on hers and her children's back she moved in with her sister. Needless to say writing took a back seat for a while. Little by little God began to help her heal and put her life back together. With nothing but time and a lot of grief she was led by the Lord to finish the book she'd started.

With Guidance from the Lord she was able to write The Power of Love series and is now a published author. Angela is a strong woman of faith and a fighter. She's currently working on the sequel to The Power of Love series and has started another new book. She also writing and producing her plays. Angela loves writing and creating new works that's filled with faith, and a strong message to heal the world of hurting men and women. She aspires to be a bestselling author and hopes to see her work on the big screen one day as well as television.

www.ingramcontent.com/pod-product-compliance
Lightning Source LLC
Chambersburg PA
CBHW071227260626
47162CB00004B/1444